# The Newcomer

*Amish Country Brides*

~

*The Prequel*

Jennifer Spredemann

© 2022

Published in Indiana by *Blessed Publishing*.

www.jenniferspredemann.com

All Scripture quotations are taken from the *King James Version* of the *Holy Bible*.

Cover design by *iCreate Designs* ©

ISBN: 978-1-940492-88-9

10 9 8 7 6 5 4 3 2 1

Get a FREE Amish story as my thank you gift
when you sign up for my newsletter here:
www.jenniferspredemann.com

# BOOKS by JENNIFER SPREDEMANN

## AMISH BY ACCIDENT TRILOGY
*Amish by Accident*
*Englisch on Purpose* (Prequel to *Amish by Accident*)
*Christmas in Paradise* (Sequel to *Amish by Accident*) (co-authored with Brandi Gabriel)

## AMISH SECRETS SERIES
*An Unforgivable Secret - Amish Secrets 1*
*A Secret Encounter - Amish Secrets 2*
*A Secret of the Heart - Amish Secrets 3*
*An Undeniable Secret - Amish Secrets 4*
*A Secret Sacrifice - Amish Secrets 5* (co-authored with Brandi Gabriel)
*A Secret of the Soul - Amish Secrets 6*
*A Secret Christmas – Amish Secrets 2.5* (co-authored with Brandi Gabriel)

## KING FAMILY SAGA (AMISH ROMANCES)
*An Amish Reward (Isaac)*
*An Amish Deception (Jacob)*
*An Amish Honor (Joseph)*
*An Amish Blessing (Ruth)*
*An Amish Betrayal (David)*

# Unofficial Glossary
## of Pennsylvania Dutch Words

*Ach* –Oh

*Aenti* –Aunt

*Boppli/Bopplin* –Baby/Babies

*Bruder/Brieder* –Brother/Brothers

*Chust* –Just

*Daed/Dat* –Dad

*Dawdi* –Grandfather

*Dawdi haus* –A small dwelling typically used for grandparents

*Denki* –Thanks

*Der Herr* –The Lord

*Dochder(n)* –Daughter(s)

*Dummkopp* –Dummy

*Englischer* –A non-Amish person

*Ferhoodled* –Crazy, scatterbrained, mind is elsewhere

*Fraa* –Wife/Missus

*G'may* –Members of an Amish fellowship

*Gott* –God

*Gross sohn* –Grandson

*Gut* –Good

*Guten tag* –Good day, good morning

*Herr* –Mister/Lord

*Jah* –Yes

*Kapp* – Amish head covering

*Kinner* –Children

*Kumm* –Come

*Maed/Maedel* –Girls/Girl

*Mamm* –Mom

*Rumspringa* –Running around period for Amish youth

*Schatzi* –Sweetheart

*Schweschder(n)* –Sister(s)

*Sohn* –Son

*Wunderbaar* – Wonderful

# Author's Note

The Amish/Mennonite people and their communities differ one from another. There are, in fact, no two Amish communities exactly alike. It is this premise on which this book is written. I have taken cautious steps to assure the authenticity of Amish practices and customs. Old Order Amish and New Order Amish may be portrayed in this work of fiction and may differ from some communities. Although the book may be set in a certain locality, the practices featured in the book may not necessarily reflect that particular district's beliefs or culture. This book is purely fictional and built around a fictional community, even though you may see similarities to real-life people, practices, and occurrences.

We, as *Englischers*, can learn a lot from the Plain People and their simple way of life. Their hard work, close-knit family life, and concern for others are to be applauded. As the Lord wills, may this special culture continue to be respected and remain so for many centuries to come, and may the light of God's salvation reach their hearts.

# ONE

"I can't believe we're actually doing this!" Excitement exploded from Josiah Beachy's voice as he bounded into Silas's bedroom and shook him by the shoulders.

Silas Miller grinned at his best friend as he attempted to fold his swim trunks and place them into his travel bag. "We are. Finally. The trip we've been talking about and planning for since...when?"

"*Ach*, didn't we talk about it when we were still in school yet?"

"*Jah*, I think so." Silas chuckled. "You've been wanting to visit the beach since Michael Eicher and his folks vacationed there."

"That's because Mike wouldn't stop talking about it. And all the pretty *maed* he saw there." Josiah's eyebrows rose twice.

"He was too young to be thinking about *maed* back then."

Josiah shrugged. "Apparently not."

Silas scratched his head. "What all should I be packing?"

"You're not taking your Amish clothes, are you?"

"I thought I would. Why?" Silas frowned.

"No pretty *Englisch* girls are going to want to hang out with Amish guys, Silas." Josiah grunted. "We need to look like *Englischers*."

"I only have one change of *Englisch* clothes. Those pants you gave me and a T-shirt."

Josiah sighed. "It looks like we'll need to do some shopping then. You don't have any shorts?"

"*Nee*. Except my swimming shorts."

"They call them swim trunks. You can't go around calling them swimming shorts."

Silas chuckled. "What does it matter what I call them?"

"*Ach*, Silas. You really need to hang out with my *Englisch* friends more."

Silas frowned. Honestly, he didn't care much for Josiah's *Englisch* friends. They tended to be rude and demeaning toward the Amish culture, which Silas happened to appreciate and respect. "No, thank you."

"*Jah*, I know Derek is a jerk. But the other guys aren't too bad."

"I don't know. I just feel like they're always trying

to pull us away. I have no intentions of jumping the fence." His gaze narrowed in on his friend. "And I hope *you* don't either."

"I'd be lying if I said I've never thought about it."

"Well, that's normal, I guess." He'd thought about it a time or two but had never truly considered it.

"Right."

"You know what they say. The grass always looks greener on the other side of the fence. It isn't really greener. It just appears to be."

"Well, I'm thinking about sand right now. Not grass." Josiah cuffed Silas on the shoulder.

Silas couldn't suppress his own enthusiasm. "Do you really think it's as great as Mike makes it out to be?"

"*Nee*. I think it's better."

"I guess we'll find out soon enough." Silas chuckled. "My brother Paul keeps begging me to take him with us."

"We're not taking any *kinner* along."

Silas folded his jeans and placed them in his luggage. "*Jah*, I know."

"What do your folks say?"

"About us going?" Silas shrugged. "*Mamm* doesn't like it one bit. *Dat* doesn't seem to have any objections."

"Your *daed's* always been cool."

Silas stared at his friend. "You think?"

"Remember when he saw us riding the neighbor's motorcycle?"

"*Ach*, I almost forgot about that."

"How could you forget? That was one of the best things we've ever done." Enthusiasm burst from Josiah's lips.

"I'm not sure the bishop would agree. Or my *mamm*."

"And your *daed* never even said anything, ain't so? Just smiled and waved at us."

"You're right. If he'd mentioned it to *Mamm*, she would have had a fit."

"A week and a half at the beach!" Josiah grasped Silas's arms and shook him. "I can hardly believe it."

Silas chuckled. *Ach*, had he ever seen his friend so excited? Not that *he* wasn't, but... "Well, we better enjoy it because we'll be needing to help your *dat* with that corn harvest when we get back."

Josiah groaned. "Why'd you have to bring that up? We're not going to talk about what awaits us when we return, okay? We're going to forget about all that and just enjoy ourselves."

"Right."

Silas's brother Paul chose that moment to sail into

his bedroom and plop onto the bed. "Ugh, y'all are so lucky! Can you find a way to hide me in your suitcase, Silas?"

Silas chuckled. "Sorry, *bruder*. No can do."

"But it's so unfair." Paul complained. "You'll be spending an entire week at the beach while I'm stuck here doing your chores."

"Week and a half, *kind*." Josiah squeezed Paul's shoulder. "You'll get your chance someday. We've waited a long time for this. We deserve it."

Silas was unsure how deserving they were. They already had so many blessings as it was. He hadn't really done anything to deserve them, except for being born at the right place at the right time to the right people. But that was something that *Der Herr* determined, not them.

"What are you going to do for *that* long?" Paul's eyes doubled in size.

Josiah's shoulders jounced. "Oh, I don't know. Meet some pretty girls, play volleyball on the beach, grab some brats and grill out, jump on the rides at the boardwalk, rent some surfboards. Those kinds of boring things."

Silas couldn't help the anticipation that rose in his chest. *Ach*, it did sound like they'd be indulging in a little slice of paradise.

"Ah, man. Now I want to go even more." A heavy sigh escaped Paul's lips.

"Well, like Josiah said, you'll get your turn someday." Silas assured him.

"*Jah*, start saving your pennies because a trip like this isn't cheap, *bu*." Josiah ruffled Paul's hair.

"I already have forty dollars saved up!" The pride in his younger brother's voice was unmistakable.

"That's a good start." Silas smiled at his *bruder*. He knew how difficult it was to save money in an Amish household when you were under twenty-one. Most of the money went to *Dat* for living expenses.

"*Jah*, but you'll need a lot more for a trip like this." Josiah turned his attention back to Silas. "Are you done yet?"

"Almost. I need a towel."

"You don't need a towel. We'll use the ones from the hotel."

"But *Mamm* said those are supposed to stay inside the hotel. We're not supposed to take them to the beach," Silas said.

"Well, you bring one if you want but I'm using the hotel's towels. That's what they're there for." Josiah insisted.

Silas wouldn't argue with his friend, even though he disagreed. Disputing about a towel seemed silly.

But he'd still be a *gut* example to his brother and do the right thing. "Paul, will you fetch my blue towel, please? The big one?"

Paul shot out of the room.

"Someday he and Jaden will be doing this. We'll probably be old and married then." Josiah mused aloud.

"Seven years? *Jah*, probably." Silas wondered who he'd end up marrying. He couldn't picture himself with any of the *maed* in his youth group. "Who do you think you'll marry?"

Josiah laughed. "I have no idea."

"What about Katie Troyer?"

"I only took her home twice. She's cute, but she's not for me." His brow arched. "What about you and Lizzie?"

Silas shook his head. "*Nee*." The woman he married would be someone he cared for in a special way. He wasn't sure what exactly he was looking for, but he knew what he wasn't. "*Der Herr* will let me know when it's the right one."

"You think so? How?"

He shrugged, chucking his shower bag into his suitcase. "I think it will feel different. You know what I mean? It'll be more than just attraction, and more than just friendship. We'll click or something."

Josiah grinned.

"What? Why are you looking at me like that?"

"Have you been reading your *mamm's* romance novels or something?" He burst into laughter.

Silas snatched a pair of socks from his bag and threw them at Josiah. "My *mamm* doesn't read romance novels. And I don't find it funny in the least. I think it will feel like I found the missing puzzle piece when I meet the right one."

The sides of Josiah's lips twitched. "Are you saying you're not complete without her?"

"Right now, I'm fine. But I suspect that when I meet her I might feel that way, *jah*." Silas laughed now too. "But I'm certainly not going to worry myself about it right now. That is *Gott's* business. I don't plan to go looking for anyone. I reckon He'll have to bring her to me and open my eyes to her."

"And I just want a girl who's hot." Josiah chuckled.

"*Jah*, but this will be the person you're spending your whole life with. Good looks and nice bodies will change. If she doesn't have a *gut* heart, then you'll end up being miserable."

"Or if she's a terrible cook," Josiah jested.

"*Nee*, then you'd just have to learn to cook for yourself. And that's probably not a bad thing to learn." When Josiah threw the socks back at him, they bounced off his chest and landed in his travel bag. "*Gut* shot."

Josiah made a show of puffing out his chest. "*Jah, vell*, when you're king of the court..."

Silas snickered. "Whatever."

"Okay, so I'm not as *gut* as you, but I did make that three-pointer."

"I remember that. A miracle, for sure." He chuckled. "Because we know it wasn't skill."

"Ouch. I plan to get some *gut* volleyball games in at the beach, though. Do you think we can find some pretty girls to play with us?"

Silas zipped up his bag. "You'll be too distracted, and we'll lose."

"Silas, Silas." Josiah shook his head and threw an arm around his friend's shoulders. "Sometimes, there are more important things than winning a game."

Silas shrugged Josiah's arm off. "I know that. I was joking."

"Maybe we'll find you a pretty *Englisch* girl too."

"I don't want an *Englisch* girl." He couldn't even picture himself with one. It would just be...awkward. And it was already awkward enough courting Amish *maed*.

"You will when you see them at the beach in their bathing suits."

"*Ach*. I'm not looking for lust. I want more out of a relationship than that. And you should too."

"Goodness, Silas. I'm not *that* shallow. Besides, you can't deny that you want your future *fraa* to be *gut* looking. I've seen your head turn a time or two when a cute girl goes by."

Paul finally entered holding the blue towel Silas had requested. "Are you guys *still* talking about *maed*?"

"Just wait a couple of years, young one." Josiah tweaked Paul's nose. "You'll be thinking and talking about girls too."

"I don't know about that." Paul shook his head. "I don't even want to think about all that boring stuff." He rolled his eyes. "I'd just want to go on the rides and swim in the ocean."

"*Ach*, how little you know." Josiah chuckled. "Women are anything but boring."

"You haven't met *mei schweschdern*, then," Paul said.

"They're young yet. Just wait a few years. I bet they'll be turning heads then."

"Whatever you say." Paul shrugged, then glanced at his brother. "Hey, Silas. Will you bring me back something special?"

Silas examined his *bruder*. "Like what?"

"Oh, I don't know. Anything, I guess."

"We'll see." Silas turned to Josiah. "What time are we leaving tomorrow?"

"Allen's picking us up around seven. He'll already have Danny with him. So, just eat something before then and we'll load up and go." Josiah laced his fingers together and cracked his knuckles. "Danny wants to get coffee on the way."

"*Ach*, I'll probably *chust* have coffee here. They charge too much at those fancy places." He mentally counted the money in his wallet. After paying his part for the hotel, and purchasing his meals, there wouldn't be too much left over for recreation. He'd have to be choosy about which amusement park rides he chose to go on.

At nineteen, he still gave most of his construction earnings to *Dat*. Fortunately, *Dat* had allowed him to save up some extra for this trip. He looked forward to the day he'd turn twenty-one and get to keep all his money. By then, maybe he'd be looking for a place of his own.

If *Mamm* and *Dat* didn't have any more male *bopplin*, their folks' place would pass on to little Nathaniel, who was only six yet. It was hard to imagine Nathaniel grown up and married and his folks with gray heads, although a few were already peeking through under *Mamm's kapp*. Unlike Josiah's folks, Alvin and Ada Beachy, who were quite a bit older in age than Silas's folks and were now fully gray.

Josiah couldn't help running the entire way to Silas's house. Allen had just called, and he'd be picking the both of them up at the Beachys' place in twenty minutes. By the time he reached the Millers' door, he was out of breath.

The door swung open before he had a chance to knock. "Josiah, you are early." Silas's *dat*, Ezra Miller, opened the door wide. "*Kumm* in, *kumm* in."

As Josiah stepped inside, Ezra stepped outside—cup of steaming coffee in one hand, Bible in the other. Silas had said his *dat* always liked to watch the sunrise from the porch while sipping a cup of coffee and talking with the Good Lord.

"Have you eaten yet?" Dorcas Miller gestured toward the table where Silas piled his plate with scrambled eggs, bread, and bacon.

He really didn't have time but… "I guess I could eat a little bit since Silas isn't ready yet." He sat next to Silas and was promptly provided with a plate and fork. "*Denki*."

Josiah bowed his head, uttered a brief silent prayer, then dug in. Judging by the quiet house, Silas and his folks were likely the only ones in the household up at this hour.

"Allen's picking us up at my place in about fifteen minutes, so we need to hurry," he mumbled around a slice of crispy bacon.

"I can take my coffee to go." Silas eyed his *mamm*. "Will you put my coffee in a thermos, please?"

"Would you like one too, Josiah?" Dorcas offered.

"*Nee, denki.* I'll grab mine on the road." He shoved a couple slices of bacon and a helping of scrambled eggs into a slice of bread and folded it like a taco. "We need to go, Silas."

"I think the *kinner* wanted to say goodbye. Or Paul did, at least." Silas stood and grasped his bag by the door. "*Mamm*, will you tell Paul and the other *kinner* goodbye for me, please? Allen's coming early."

"Do you have everything you need, *sohn*?"

"I think so."

"On your way out, holler to your *dat* that his breakfast is ready."

"*Jah*, okay, *Mamm*. Goodbye." Silas donned his hat, even though he wouldn't be wearing it when they went to the beach. It was likely a formality for his folks' sake.

Josiah almost protested but didn't want to earn one of Dorcas's scowls. "We should probably hurry."

"*Ach*, it won't hurt Allen and Danny to learn a little patience. It's not like they're going to leave without us, right?"

"You have a point. Besides, if we run, it'll make my side ache after eating your *mamm's* breakfast. That bacon was amazing."

"Wasn't it? Her bacon is the best. I don't know what she does that's different than other people."

"Wanna race to my house?" Josiah asked.

"I thought you said your side would ache?"

"I'm *gut* now. And I might actually have a chance of winning since you're carrying your bag."

Silas snorted, his eyes sparkling with mirth. "Okay, you're on."

# TWO

"We're here!"

Silas's eyes flew open at the sound of Josiah's voice as his head knocked against the doorframe at the same time. Josiah's hand shook his shoulder, bringing him back to full consciousness.

"Sorry, speed bump." Allen grimaced.

Silas's gaze went to the tall hotel building as Allen maneuvered the vehicle into a parking space.

"We can see the beach from the other side." Josiah informed him. "We asked for rooms that looked out over the ocean."

*Jah*, Josiah had to choose one of the more expensive establishments, to Silas's annoyance, but he rolled with it anyway. After all, it wasn't like they'd ever be doing this again.

*Ach*, he could hardly believe they'd arrived. Ten days of nothing but fun and recreation. It almost seemed sinful, to his thinking. As a matter of fact, he felt guilty leaving all the work at home for *Dat* and the boys. But he wouldn't think about that now. Besides, *Dat* had encouraged him to come and enjoy himself.

"Leave your stuff in the car until we figure out where our rooms will be." Danny opened the passenger door and stepped out.

Silas and Josiah vacated the backseat. *Ach*, it felt so *gut* to stretch his legs.

"The hotel said that we could check in early when I called for reservations." Josiah grinned.

After checking in and receiving their room assignments, Silas and Josiah dropped their belongings off in their room.

"I'm going to see if Danny and Allen want to go to the boardwalk. Does that sound *gut* to you?" Glancing back at Silas, he twisted the doorknob.

"*Jah*. Are we going on rides today?"

Josiah shrugged. "Maybe. I thought we'd *chust* go over there and check it out. See how much everything costs."

"That sounds *gut*. I need to find something for Paul and the other *kinner*, so maybe I can get something for them today. I don't want to forget."

"It's a plan. I'll be right back."

As soon as Josiah disappeared, Silas plopped down

on the bed, leaned back, and closed his eyes. "*Gott, denki* for giving us this opportunity. Please help me be pleasing to You and not get caught up in doing things that will make You frown."

He thought about that for a moment. Did *Der Herr* ever frown? A verse that *Dat* had read a few times came to mind about *Gott* being angry with the wicked every day. *Jah*, he supposed *Gott* probably did frown. And if He knew how wicked this world was getting, Silas suspected that *Gott* might frown quite a bit.

Resolve surged in Silas's gut, and he determined to do what he could to make *Gott* smile. He liked the picture of a smiling *Gott* much better than the picture of an angry *Gott*.

Josiah reentered the room with two beer bottles in his hands. He took a swig of the open one and handed the other one to Silas.

His first test, it seemed. "*Nee, denki*." Silas shook his head.

"*Kumm* on, Silas. We're on a holiday. Our folks aren't here."

"I don't want any." He insisted. "You know I don't care for that stuff."

"*Jah*, but I thought you *chust* said that because you didn't want to get in trouble." He downed another drink.

17

"*Nee.*" Besides, he'd just told *Der Herr* he wanted to please Him. Somehow, going against his folks' wishes and the laws of the land didn't seem like something *Gott* would be pleased with.

Josiah shrugged. "Suit yourself. More for me, I guess." He opened the fridge and set the extra bottle inside.

"When are we going to the boardwalk?" Not that he was changing the subject…okay, maybe he was purposely changing the subject, but he *was* curious about their activities today.

"Ten minutes. We'll walk down on the beach."

Silas smiled. "That sounds *gut*. I can't wait to feel the sand and the water."

"*Chust* don't drink any of the water. It's salty."

"How do you know?"

"Mike Eicher said he tried to surf out there and nearly drowned." Josiah chuckled. "Anyway, he said he swallowed a bunch of water and it was nasty."

"You don't believe he almost drowned?" Silas frowned.

"You know Mike. You don't know when you can believe him." Josiah shook his head. "Like that *Englisch* girlfriend he said he'd had."

"I thought that's why he left. Because of the girlfriend."

"*Nee*, he was upset with his folks over something. He wouldn't talk to me about it, so I don't know what was going on with him."

"I thought he talked to you about everything."

"Not that. He *chust* took off." Josiah shrugged. "He has a *grossdawdi* in Indiana, so maybe he went there. Either that, or he's *Englisch* now. I plan to try to find him one of these days."

Silas wasn't sure if that was a wise course of action for his best friend. Michael tended to lead him off in the wrong direction. Silas feared that one day Michael might persuade Josiah to leave their people. If that ever happened, he'd be devastated.

He'd always had hopes of the two of them buying property next to each other and raising their families as next-door neighbors like they'd been raised. If Mike persuaded Josiah to leave, Silas would be lonely for sure.

If Silas admitted it to himself, he was kind of glad when Michael left Pennsylvania. Because now, Michael wouldn't be influencing Josiah to do things he shouldn't do. He eyed the bottle in his friend's hand. He wasn't sure Allen and Danny were *gut* influences for his friend either.

He'd have to remember to say an extra prayer for all of them tonight.

Silas couldn't erase his smile as his toes sank into the soft, warm sand. As their group moved toward the ocean, the water gently lapped at his feet. He could easily see why folks loved the beach so much. There was just something about it. It was relaxing. The ocean seemed to bring a calm to his soul. It was as if the waves could wash away any anxiety one was feeling.

It was no wonder people referred to tropical places as paradise. And this place wasn't even tropical. How much more lovely could an island be? To Silas's thinking, it couldn't get much better than this.

He suddenly wished his family could be here to enjoy this too. He knew Paul would especially love it. They all would, except maybe the *boppli*, Emily. She'd be too young to even know. Maybe someday they could all come and enjoy a week here. And it would be even better if Josiah's family could come along as well.

"What do you think of suggesting to our folks that we come here for a holiday?" He voiced his thoughts to Josiah, then glanced up ahead where their two friends had meandered.

"You mean bring our whole families?"

Silas nodded. "I think they'd enjoy it. Don't you?"

"*Jah*, probably. Maybe sometime after harvest when we aren't too busy." Josiah's lips twisted. "*Jah*, I think Jaden, Justin, and Joshua would have a *gut* time.

Especially if your *schweschdern* come along."

"*Mei schweschdern*?" His lips turned downward.

"I think *mei bruder* might have a thing for Martha." Josiah smiled.

"Jaden?"

He nodded. "You know how quiet he is. When Martha's name comes up, his face lights up and he always has something nice to say about her."

Silas frowned now and a surge of overprotectiveness filled him. "They're too young. They better not be doing anything."

"Goodness, Silas. It's not like they're courting."

His fist clenched. "Do you know if she likes him too?"

"I wouldn't know. Why don't you ask her when we get home?"

"*Jah*, I think I'll do that."

Josiah pointed up ahead of them. "There's the boardwalk!"

Silas whistled low as his eyes zeroed in on a rollercoaster in the distance. "Look at that! Are we going to try it?"

"You bet! I can't wait."

"How much do you think it will cost?"

"I'm not sure. I'm hoping they have an all-day pass we can buy."

"But that would only be *gut* for a day, ain't so? It might be better to *chust* pay for each thing."

"We'll figure it out when we get there. I think Danny said it's like ten dollars to go on the rollercoaster."

"Ten dollars?" He hadn't meant to raise his voice, but goodness... At that rate, his money would be gone in no time.

"I don't think the other rides are that much."

"I hope not. Because after going on rides and buying food, I'll run out of money before our trip is half over."

"*Jah*, I know what you mean."

# THREE

Josiah's head snapped backward as the pretty blonde passed him on the boardwalk once again. The second time in the last half hour. He was certain their eyes had connected this time. *Ach*, he needed to meet her.

He became deaf to Silas's words as he formulated a plan in his mind. He couldn't follow her around. If he did, she would probably think he was creepy. But what if they casually met to where it seemed like a coincidence?

"What were you looking at?"

"*Ach*, nothing." He glanced back again just as he saw the young woman get in line for the rollercoaster. "I want to go on the rollercoaster again," he blurted out. He turned an about face and headed in the direction they'd just come from.

Silas frowned and attempted to keep up with his

brisk pace. "But we already went on it. And it was expensive. I thought you said—"

"Never mind what I said. *Kumm* on." He needed to get in line behind her before someone else did.

"I'm not going on it again." Silas insisted.

"That's fine. You can sit on that bench over there." He abandoned his friend and tried to rush to the end of the line without seeming obvious. Unfortunately, there were several people who had beat him to the line and now stood between him and the pretty girl.

He blew out his breath. When and if he got the chance, how would he engage with her? Would he even get a chance?

At that moment, she glanced back, and he smiled. When she smiled back, it nearly knocked him off his feet. *Ach*, she had a gorgeous smile.

Too bad she turned back around. He sighed. *Gott, please give me a chance to talk to her.* He wasn't sure *Der Herr* would be all that keen on answering his prayers since he rarely sent words upward, but it was worth a shot.

Just from what he'd seen of her so far, he imagined her to be a sweet person. She didn't seem like those girls who had their noses stuck up in the air and thought they were too good for you. For that, he was thankful. Of course, he knew nothing about her, so he hoped his assumptions were correct.

As the line moved forward, he caught her eye a couple more times. He probably seemed too obvious, but he couldn't help it. He was afraid that if he took his eyes off her she would disappear again.

He hoped she didn't mind. But she had glanced his way too, so he was pretty certain the attraction wasn't one-sided.

As he approached the front of the line, she hurried to claim the first seat. The people in front of him moved in the opposite direction, but when it came up to his turn, all the seats were full. Which meant he'd have to wait until the next ride. Which meant she would be getting off when he was still riding. Which meant she'd probably disappear into the crowd, and he'd never see her again.

The attendant went around making sure the riders' safety belts were secure.

He squeezed his eyes closed for a brief moment. *Gott, please.* When he opened them, he noticed the attendant was bent over conversing with the young woman. Likely flirting with her. He sighed.

The same attendant then approached him. "The young woman in the front car said you're welcome to ride in the empty seat next to her."

*Ach*, had he heard right? "She offered to let me ride with her?"

He glanced her way, and she flashed a shy smile. *Denki, Gott!*

"You need to be quick," the attendant urged.

Without another second, he nodded and rushed to the rollercoaster's front car. The attendant waited until he clicked his safety belt on, then he lowered a metal bar in front of them. As the attendant moved to the cars behind them, Josiah glanced at his fellow passenger.

"Hi." Her cheeks turned a gentle shade of pink.

"Hi. Thank you for letting me ride with you."

She shrugged. "I was riding alone, so might as well, right?"

He nodded. "My name is Josiah Beachy," he said, in hopes she'd share her name.

"Beachy? Like the beach? That's so cool."

"Do you think so?"

"Unless you're making it up." She studied him closely.

He chuckled. "No, that's my name."

"I'm Kayla Johnson."

*Ach*, Kayla. What a lovely name. He wasn't sure if he'd heard of anyone by that name. There was no one in his community with that name, he knew. It fit her well. "I like your name."

"It's okay, I guess." The rollercoaster began moving forward and she gripped the metal bar holding them in. "Are you ready? I've got to warn you, I'll probably scream."

He glanced at her and laughed. "I might too." He gripped the metal bar tightly as well.

For the rest of the ride, neither of them spoke because they were too focused on holding on for dear life as the rollercoaster veered around corners, moved through twists and turns, and careened down steep drops at heart-pounding speeds.

When it finally came to a stop, they both laughed.

"That was a blast." He didn't think her grin could get any wider.

"Wasn't it?"

After the attendant lifted the metal restraint, they unfastened their seatbelts.

"Where are you going now?" he asked.

She flashed her perfect teeth. "I have a few more rides I planned to go on. Have you been on the Ferris wheel yet?"

"No." He was pretty sure Silas had said he didn't want to ride on that one. "Do you want company? I'm here with my friend, but I don't think he planned on riding the Ferris wheel."

Pleasure lit up her face. "I'd love company."

They maneuvered their way out of the exit line.

"Just a minute. If you wait right here, I'll go talk to

my friend and see what he says." Josiah hurried over to the bench Silas sat on. "Hey, do you mind if I take a ride on the Ferris wheel?"

"Sure. I can stay here. Maybe I'll grab a snack or look for those souvenirs I wanted to get."

"Okay. Good idea. What if I meet you back at the bench in about twenty minutes? Maybe thirty, depending on if there's a line for the Ferris wheel. Will that work for you?"

"That sounds *gut*." Silas nodded.

"Awesome." Josiah squeezed his friend's shoulder, then made his way back to the pretty girl waiting for him. "Okay, we're good. He's going to hang out and maybe get a bite to eat."

"Oh. Well, I hate to interrupt your time with your friend. Are you sure he's okay with it?"

"Yes, he's good. I told him I'd be back in twenty to thirty minutes, so we might have time for a couple of rides if you want company for a little bit."

"Really? That was nice of him to agree. I feel kind of bad, like I'm taking you away from your friend."

"Nah, he's fine. Don't worry about him." He studied her a moment. "What about you? Aren't you here with someone?" Like a boyfriend?

"I'm in Ocean City with my parents but riding the rides on my own."

"Just you and your folks?"

"Yes." She glanced at him as they made their way toward the Ferris wheel. "What about you? Is it just you and your friend?"

"There are four of us guys here."

"So, is this like a party trip?"

"Sort of, I guess." He shrugged. "It's actually my first time coming to the ocean."

Her eyes lit up and her mouth dropped open. "Your very first time? Really?"

"Yep."

"What do you think of it?"

"*Ach*, it's amazing. Beautiful. So much more than I thought it would be."

"I know, right? The ocean is one of my most favorite places in the world." They both stepped in line for the ride, then she turned back to him. "So, your first time. Wow. How old are you?"

"I'm nineteen."

She nodded. "That's about what I figured you to be."

"What about you? How old are you?"

Fortunately, the attendant interrupted their conversation by pointing them to an open carriage on the Ferris wheel.

Kayla pondered what she would say to this handsome guy. If she told him she'd just turned sixteen, he'd likely write her off as too young. There was no way she was going to chance that after she finally got to meet and talk to him. He was one of the cutest guys she'd ever seen, and he seemed to be interested. She'd be stupid to blow her chances with him.

After they were fastened in, he turned to her. "You're how old?"

"Eighteen." She squeaked out. She hated lying and felt guilty for deceiving him.

He seemed to relax after that. "Good. Not too young."

Her heartbeat sped up. She'd been right. He probably would have said adios after the ride was over if she'd spilled the truth.

His hand inched closer to hers. "Do you mind?"

She shook her head, and his hand covered hers over the safety bar. She was almost certain the pounding in her chest could be heard audibly. The visible veins and strength in his hand told her he was probably a hard worker. They weren't soft like someone who worked an office job. Not that the men who worked office jobs weren't hard workers. But by the way he was put together, she could tell he probably did a lot of physical labor. He was more solid than the guys she went to school with.

"What are your plans after you're done on the rides?" Did he want to spend more time together? He shot her that smile that made her insides get all mushy. She could hardly believe a guy like this would be interested in her.

"My schedule is pretty much open, but my parents will want me to have dinner with them tonight."

He nodded. "And what about tomorrow?"

"I was thinking about laying out to try to get a tan. Then I might go boogie boarding." Her heart leaped as the Ferris wheel began turning.

"Boogie boarding? What's that?"

Oh wow. He'd never heard of boogie boarding? She knew he wasn't from the west coast by his unique accent, but she couldn't decipher where he was from.

"Oh, my goodness, it's so much fun. You have to try it. You take your board out into the ocean and ride the waves back to the shore. There isn't really a learning curve to it like surfing, unless you want to do fancy stuff."

He laughed. "You'll need to show me for sure."

"I'll be glad to have someone to ride with. But you'll need to either rent or buy a boogie board." When they reached the top, she looked out at the boardwalk and took in the ocean view. It was all so romantic, especially with Josiah here next to her, lavishing all this attention on her. She felt special.

"Do you have one of these boards?"

"Yes, at home. But I didn't bring it with me, so I'll rent one."

"I guess I'll rent one too, then. Do you know what it costs?"

She shrugged. "I'm not exactly sure. Maybe like ten or fifteen dollars a day? If you're going to rent one for several days, you'd be better off just buying one because they're not that expensive."

"I wouldn't have use for it after this trip."

She pondered his words. "What do you do for a living?"

"I work on my dad's farm."

"No wonder."

"What do you mean?"

Her face heated. "I figured you did some type of manual labor." Her eyes gave him a once-over.

"You figured right, then." He intertwined his fingers with hers. "What time do you want to go tomorrow and where should we meet?"

"Where are you staying?"

He gave her the name of the hotel and she recognized it as one of the establishments close to where she was staying with her parents.

"I could meet you outside the entrance at maybe ten thirty. Would that work for you?"

"That sounds wonderful. I'll be there at ten thirty."

Kayla's heart soared as she thought about spending time with Josiah again.

It almost seemed like a date.

# FOUR

"Where are you going?" Silas's brow lowered as he watched his friend abandon their volleyball game. He quickened his pace to keep up with him as their feet sank into the sand with each step.

Josiah's grin widened. "Sorry, but I've got a date."

"The girl you went on the Ferris wheel with yesterday?"

"That's the one." His eyebrows raised and lowered twice. "Oh, man, Silas. She is...amazing. Beautiful. She's a dream, really."

"And you know that after spending thirty minutes with her?"

"Absolutely. When you know, you know."

What on earth was his friend talking about?

"You know what?"

"I think I might be in love with her."

Silas couldn't help the snort that escaped.

"Laugh all you want, but you'll see. She's like no one I've ever known."

"But she's *Englisch*?"

"*Jah*, she's *Englisch*." Josiah released a satisfied sigh, as if this was a *gut* thing. It wasn't.

A rock formed in Silas's gut. "You can't be in love with an *Englischer*."

"Why not?"

"There's a hundred reasons and I think you know them all. Where does she even live?" *Ach*, this was terrible.

"I honestly have no idea. We haven't gotten that far yet."

"She'd have to join the *g'may* and you know that's not easy for an *Englischer*. You better let her know what she's getting into."

"Relax, Silas. I haven't even kissed her yet."

"And you plan to?"

"*Ach*, I hope to. Ah, man. Kissing her would be so amazing." He wore a stupid grin. Josiah stopped and pointed to Allen and Danny. "I think they're waiting for you."

Why did he feel like he was being dismissed? "*Jah*, okay. When will you be back?"

"I don't know. Maybe for supper?"

"Okay. Have fun."

"There's no doubt in my mind that I will."

Kayla's heartbeat sped up the moment Josiah exited the doors from the hotel lobby. His dark hair was slightly askew and appeared damp like he'd just taken a shower. Goodness, she couldn't get over how good-looking he was. He was exactly how she pictured her dream guy.

The moment he smiled and caught her eye, she couldn't help but grin back. She was still having a hard time believing that this handsome man that could probably have any girl he wanted was spending time with her. Not only that, but he looked at her as though she was the most beautiful girl in the world.

"Hi again."

She found her voice. "Hi." She suddenly felt shy.

"Are you going to show me these boards you were talking about?"

"Boogie boards. Yes, we need to find a rental place. I think I saw a surf shop earlier that had a sign for rentals. The nice part is that the water is warm enough here to where we won't need to rent wetsuits too."

He frowned. "Wetsuits?"

Had he never seen a wetsuit either? "All the surfers

wear them at the beach I usually go to, because the water is so cold."

"I see. I think." He chuckled.

"They should have some at the surf shop. I'll show you what they look like."

"Okay."

She led the way down the sidewalk. Today was going to be so much fun. "How long do you want to be in the water for?"

He shrugged. "I don't know. How long do you usually go for?"

"Maybe an hour or two. Since lunchtime isn't too far away, we'll probably want to stop or take a break to get something to eat. What time do you usually have lunch?"

"Around noon, but it doesn't really matter to me."

"We can just go in whenever then. Do you have any other plans today?"

"No, not really. I told my friend that I'd probably be back for supper."

"Oh, good. That gives us time to hang out, if you want."

He reached for her hand and intertwined their fingers. "I want."

The wink he shot her way sent her heart galloping into next Tuesday.

Josiah stared. He couldn't help it. He was mesmerized by the beautiful woman on the boogie board beside him. Not only was she gorgeous, but she was super smart, to his thinking.

He'd never considered himself dumb, but Kayla knew about so many things that he'd never even heard of. He wished he knew more so he could understand her world better.

"What do you think of renting a bike one of these days?" She turned her board toward the shore, and he followed her lead.

"A bicycle?" He began paddling like she'd showed him when they'd taken their first plunge into the water.

"Yes, they have rentals on the boardwalk. It might be fun."

The wave came too quickly, and they both missed it.

"Aww." Kayla stared after the wave.

Thanks to his *Englisch* friends, he knew how to ride a bicycle. "We'll see."

He'd brought plenty of money for the trip, but at this rate, it would disappear quickly. He didn't mind spending *all* his money on Kayla, though. His time with her was worth every penny.

"Are you having fun?" She glanced at him before another wave passed them by.

"The best time." He moved a strand of wet hair from her face.

"We can stay as long as you'd like. I'm having fun too."

"Did you have something else in mind to do?"

"I thought it might be fun to walk through the arcade." She smiled. "I love that there's so much to do here."

"What about your folks? They don't mind if you're off doing things without them?" He'd been wondering.

"They're not around. This is a business trip for my dad so he's in and out of meetings all week. The company didn't mind him bringing my mom along to the meetings. I didn't want to stay home because my best friend is touring colleges all week and I thought I'd be bored. So I decided to come along on the trip, but I didn't want to be stuck in a hotel room all day. That's why we're *here* specifically. The only reason we're staying in Ocean City is because of me, so I'd have *something* to do."

"I see. And what about your brothers and sisters?"

"I'm an only child." She smiled. "I'm guessing you're not?"

He chuckled. "Hardly. I have eight siblings."

Her jaw dropped. "So, your parents had nine

children? Oh wow, I can't even imagine that."

It was normal, to his thinking, although Silas's folks only had six *kinner* yet. But Silas's folks were quite a bit younger than his parents so they could still have many more.

"Where are you in the line-up?"

"I'm the middle child. Two older sisters and brothers, one younger sister, and three younger brothers."

"Three girls and six boys." She shook her head. "Wow. Your mom must be some woman."

A wave came just then and they both paddled, caught it, and rode it into shore.

"Are you getting hungry? I feel like I could eat a bear."

She laughed. "That's some appetite. Ocean activities do tend to work up an appetite."

"How long have we been out here?"

"I'm thinking at least an hour and a half. Lunch does sound good." She stood and picked up her board. "Let's go."

# FIVE

After a delicious lunch with the most wonderful woman he'd ever met, Josiah let Kayla talk him into hanging out in the arcade. Honestly, he was so smitten with her that he'd probably just sit and stare at the wall, if that was what she wanted to do.

As they maneuvered their way around various games, Kayla pulled him toward a tall metal box - looking thing. Josiah had no idea what it was. He eyed the short curtain at the top of a rectangular opening. Then he noticed the round stool inside. Black and white strips of photographs were displayed on the outside along with a mirror.

"Come on, let's take pictures!" Kayla's smile beamed. *Ach*, she was so gorgeous. He still had a hard time believing she'd been spending time with him.

His brow lowered. "Pictures?"

She laughed. "Yeah, it's a photo booth."

"I'm not sure I know what that is." His lips twisted.

"I can't believe you've never seen a photo booth. Oh, they're so much fun! They have them at the fair. Every year, me and my friends take pictures in them. It's a fun memento. Come on."

*Photos?* His face warmed. He knew he was in *rumspringa* but... "I don't...I'm not really a picture person."

Her eyes scanned him up and down and a gentle smile tugged at her lips. "Oh, you're definitely a picture person."

She shook her head at his protest and drew him into the booth. "Come on. Sit down."

"Sit down?" He did as told. The booth was so small. He had no idea how they both—

She sat on his lap and stared at a rectangular piece of glass across from where they sat. Goodness gracious, did she have *any* idea what that did to him? It was like his whole body sparked to life all at once.

"No. Get up." She hopped off his lap.

*Nee*, apparently, she wasn't feeling the same thing. This woman. *Ach*. What had she said? "Get up?"

"Your puzzled expression is so cute." She pointed at the glass. "The camera is in there," she explained, pulling him up from the stool. "This has to be adjusted so that when we're sitting on it, our eye level comes to here." She showed him a line next to the camera glass, then began turning the seat to lower it.

"I see."

"Now, let's sit back down and see if that will work." She smiled as her hands pushed his shoulders down. She slid back onto his lap.

It took everything in him not to pull her close and kiss her senseless.

"Okay, this is perfect. Now, when I put the money in, we're going to get four chances to take a good picture. Let's just smile on the first two, so we'll hopefully have some nice ones, then we'll do a funny face."

That was three. "What about the last one?"

She shrugged. "We'll figure it out. Something spontaneous." Something mischievous sparkled in her eye.

"*Jah*. Okay."

"Ready?" She waited for his nod, then fed the money into the machine. "Okay, smile."

He did as she said. Why did he feel nervous? A bright light flashed in his face, and he closed his eyes.

"No, don't!" It was too late. Another flash. "Silly face."

He stuck his tongue out and raised his eyebrows.

"Now." Without warning, she lifted his chin and bent to meet his lips. Her kiss was slow and sweet. Her lips were so soft. He lifted his hand, slipping his fingers into her hair and deepened the kiss, hoping it would never have to end.

He groaned when she leaned back and giggled. "I think our photos might be ready. We usually have to wait, but—"

He couldn't help pulling her close again. This time, his hand went around her waist and her fingers tantalized the hair at the nape of his neck. He finally tore himself away when he realized someone was outside the booth waiting to use it.

"I could do that all day," he murmured, staring at her now-full pink lips. This girl was beyond his wildest dreams. Michael had been *so* right.

She reluctantly stood and dipped her head as they exited the booth. Neither one of them made eye contact with the two girls waiting outside.

The girls giggled at the sight of them and pointed to the pictures. "They've been ready for a while now."

Kayla snatched the pictures from the holder and held them to her chest as they walked away, leaving the booth to the girls.

"Aren't we going to look at them?"

Kayla stopped walking and turned. She stared into his eyes. Her chin trembled. "I think I'm in love with you."

*Ach.* His thumb grazed her cheek, removing a tear. Then he brought her close, not caring that they were surrounded by people, and gently kissed her lips. He broke the connection and gazed into her eyes. "I feel the same way."

"Yeah, but I live in California!" she cried.

"California? Like, the state? All the way on the other side of the country?" He had to clarify because he had heard of cities called by the same name.

"That's the one." She nodded. "And you live in...?"

"Pennsylvania." He sighed. *Jah*, it was a long way. Too many miles apart.

"We'll never see each other again."

"Sure, we will. Somehow." He hated that she looked so sad. "Besides, I'll be here for another eight days."

"I'm leaving in five."

"Well, then let's make the most of it. We still have four days together, right?" He didn't know how he was going to tell Silas that he wouldn't be hanging out with him and the guys as much as they'd planned. Maybe he could work out a schedule to include time with both Kayla and with his friends.

"Right."

A couple of hours later, Josiah dropped Kayla off at her hotel's lobby. He'd been tempted to pull her close and kiss her again, but there were people around and it felt awkward. "Do you want to meet again tomorrow?"

"Of course." Love sparkled in her eyes.

He knew how she felt. He could probably spend every moment of his *rumspringa* trip with her, but he was sure Silas and the guys wouldn't appreciate it. "I'd be having supper with you but—"

"No, you're here with your friends. You need to spend time with them too. I totally understand that. Besides, my parents will be coming back this evening and they won't leave until morning."

He stared at her, not wanting to leave. "I wish I didn't have to go."

*Then stay.* Kayla felt like saying it aloud, but she didn't.

Saying goodbye was always the hardest part. She knew that when she left in a few days, she'd be leaving a piece of her heart with Josiah.

"Walk me to the elevator?" It would only require another minute or so, but it was better than nothing.

He nodded and they walked hand-in-hand and down the hallway. They could have used the main elevator near the lobby, but they'd have more privacy if they didn't.

She sighed when they reached their destination. Fortunately, no one was around.

Josiah lifted his hand and caressed her cheek. "Dream about me tonight?"

"I hope I do." She'd definitely be daydreaming about him and reliving their time together. She leaned into his touch and their lips met.

When the elevator dinged, they sprung apart. Josiah released her and she stepped inside, then pushed the button for the correct floor. They stared at each other in aching silence as the elevator doors closed.

# SIX

"Wait!" Just in time, Josiah's hand stopped the doors from closing.

Kayla looked pleased that he didn't want to part ways with her. "What? What is it?"

"I have an idea." He rushed on. "Do you think you can get away tonight?"

"Tonight? What time?"

"I was thinking after everyone else has gone to sleep. What time do your folks go to bed?"

"Probably around ten." She grimaced.

"What if I meet you in the lobby of your hotel about eleven?"

She nibbled on her fingernail. "What would we do at that hour? I don't think anything is open."

"I thought it might be nice to take a walk on the beach with only the light of the moon as our guide. Maybe we could make a little fire too." Excitement stirred just imagining it.

Her lips tipped upward. "That sounds nice."

"Doesn't it?"

"I don't..." She shook her head. "What if we get caught?"

"I'll take all the blame. It's my idea, right?" Although meeting her folks for the first time would be much more pleasant if they weren't in an angry state of mind.

"Yeah, but I don't know how my parents would react if they knew I was sneaking out."

"Would you want to ask them, then?"

She shook her head. "No, I better not ask."

"Are they heavy sleepers?"

"They are, but sometimes they get up in the middle of the night. They probably wouldn't think to check my bed, though. I just...I don't know if I'll be able to leave and reenter the room without waking them."

"Well, it's totally up to you. We don't have to. I just thought a walk on the beach sounded..." He shrugged. "Romantic."

A beautiful smile lit up her face. She liked his idea. "Okay, I'll meet you. If I don't show up by eleven thirty, then you can assume I got caught sneaking out."

"If you're sure?"

"My dad is always telling me I should do spontaneous things. That will be my alibi."

He wasn't sure what alibi meant, but he wasn't about to risk sounding *dumm* in front of this amazing girl. "Okay. Eleven it is, then." He couldn't wipe his silly grin off his face if he tried.

Now, to plan for the evening.

Silas eyed Josiah from across the table as they shared supper with Danny and Allen.

"We rented a movie and bought some snacks. You two want to join us for a little partying tonight?" Allen grinned.

Silas grunted inwardly. He enjoyed his friends' company, but when they mentioned "partying" he knew that meant alcohol would be involved. Ever since one of the members of their *g'may* was senselessly killed while under the influence of alcohol, Silas had decided to swear off drinking. From what he could see, *gut* never seemed to come from it. It tended to make people act stupid.

Silas glanced at Josiah and raised a brow.

"What?" Josiah blinked.

Danny laughed. "I don't think he heard a word Allen said."

"About what?" Josiah asked.

They all laughed.

"*Nee*, he's daydreaming about that *Englisch* girl he met." Allen teased.

Silas frowned. He loved Josiah, but his friend tended to think with his heart instead of his head sometimes. He was afraid of the influence this *Englisch* girl might have on him.

A lazy smile formed on Josiah's lips. "I have a date tonight."

Danny whistled low. "Must be some girl."

Silas glanced at the clock on the restaurant wall. It was almost eight o'clock.

"She's crazy hot." Josiah waggled his eyebrows.

"Well, I don't blame you, then. Does she have a friend, by the way?" Allen chuckled.

"No."

"You've been with her most of the day, ain't not?" Silas protested.

"Don't worry, friend. You've got me for the rest of the evening." Josiah squeezed his shoulder. "You'll be sleeping like a baby when I leave."

"What time is your date?" Danny's expression widened.

"Eleven." Josiah smirked. "Man, I can't wait."

"You're a lucky man." Danny laughed.

"That reminds me. I have some preparing to do." Josiah glanced at Silas. "Wanna help me put up a tent?"

"A tent?" Silas blinked.

"Where else are they gonna *sleep*? You want him to bring her to your hotel room?" Allen laughed.

Josiah frowned. "Hey, easy." He glanced at Silas. "I'm not planning to sleep with her."

Silas released a brief sigh of relief. He had no desire to be a party to sin, if that was what his friend had in mind. "*Jah*, I'll help."

# SEVEN

As soon as Kayla entered the lobby, she spotted Josiah lounging on one of the cozy couches, a cup of complimentary water in his hand.

"Sorry, I'm a little late." She hurried over to him, then glanced around. They were the only people in the lobby at this hour. Even the front desk staff seemed to have disappeared.

"Did you get into trouble?" Concern filled his features as he studied her intently and gently grasped her wrist.

"No, nothing like that. It's just that my dad was sleeping, but he rolled over and stopped snoring. So, I just sat there waiting until he finally started again." She grimaced. "I just hope they didn't wake up when the door clicked shut. I wish they made those things silent."

"I know. It would make escaping much easier." His wink sent her heart skittering.

She glanced back toward the elevator. "Well, no sign of them so we're probably safe."

"How do you plan on slipping back in without them knowing?"

"I think that part will be easier. I'll just request an extra blanket from the front desk and bring it back to the room with me. I'll tell them I got cold, which is true. My dad sets the AC way colder than it needs to be and it's freezing in there. I guess he's not used to the humidity here."

"It's not humid in California?"

"Hardly. We get a lot of sunshine, but not a lot of rain."

"I see." His handsome brow lifted. "You ready to go?"

All of a sudden, excitement filled her and she felt giddy. "I'm ready."

His palm slid against hers and they exited the hotel hand-in-hand.

As Josiah led Kayla out to the beach, she slipped off her sandals and walked barefoot through the cool sand. The beautiful medley of the ocean waves lapping against the shore and the moon sparkling off the water nearly took her breath away.

"I brought a flashlight in case the moon decides to

hide behind the clouds." Josiah clicked on the light and that was when she discovered a tent and two chairs around what appeared to be a makeshift fire pit.

"What is *this* all about?" Admiration filled Kayla's heart at the sight before her.

"I thought I'd bring out the tent." He shrugged. "If the wind picks up or it rains and we need shelter, then we're all set. Besides, I brought something."

Josiah dashed into the tent and brought out a plastic grocery bag. There was enough moonlight to see the bag of marshmallows, two chocolate bars, and the box of graham crackers he'd handed her.

Happiness filled Kayla's heart. "S'mores!"

"Do you like it?" There'd been a hint of hopefulness in his voice. Had he doubted?

"What's not to like? Josiah, you're amazing. Of course. I love it." She stood on tiptoes and grazed his cheek with a kiss.

"I figured we could take a walk down the shore first, then come back and make a little fire. Maybe we'll find some driftwood to use to start it, although I did bring some kindling and a little wood."

"Wow, you've thought of everything." Not only was Josiah Beachy crazy handsome, but he was also thoughtful and romantic. A girl could swoon over a guy like that.

"I want this night to be one you'll always remember. I don't want you to forget me when you go back home to California."

She shook her head. "I don't think I'll *ever* be able to forget you, Josiah Beachy." She didn't want to think about going back to California. Her heart ached at the thought of them parting ways in a few days. If only she could stay here with him. If only there was a way for them to be together.

It was an impossible dream, and she knew it. But she'd also heard that love could conquer anything. Could she and Josiah somehow make a long-distance relationship between them work?

He stepped near and cradled her face in his hands. "And neither will I forget you."

"It's going to be hard to leave." She swallowed down her emotion.

"I know." He placed the sweetest kiss on her lips, then stepped back and reached for her hand. "Come, let's enjoy the time we do have together."

They walked in companionable silence for several minutes. She guessed his mind was probably turning as much as hers had been.

He slipped an arm around her waist. "Do your parents have meetings again tomorrow?"

"Yes."

"What do you think of having breakfast together?"

"Our hotel usually has a continental breakfast."

"So does ours." He grinned. "I have an idea. What if I grab a plate from my hotel and you grab a plate from yours, and we can share and eat together? We just need to figure out where."

"Well, my parents will be gone so we could go back to our hotel room. There's a table and chairs in the room and it will be perfect for that."

Excitement surged in his gut. "That sounds like a plan. What time?"

"They leave at like seven thirty, so any time after that." They'd already walked down the shore a ways, so they turned a loop and began their journey back.

"Is eight thirty good?"

She nodded and he noticed the moon highlighting her white teeth. "Sounds good to me. But what about your friends?"

"We've got a volleyball game planned in the late morning and they want to grill out for lunch, so we're good until then."

"That will give me time to work on my tan."

"Do you want to meet my friends?" Now, why did he go and say that? Surely they'd give his Amishness away. He wondered if she'd even be spending time with him if she knew the truth. *Please let her say no.*

"I don't know." Her nose wrinkled. "That's your guy time. You came with them, so I'm sure they want you with them at least some of the time."

"You're right. You don't have to. It might be kind of awkward, anyhow." Especially if they were drinking. He needed to change the subject quick. "What about supper then? Are you free for supper?"

"I'm not sure what time my parents will be back tomorrow. I'll have to ask them in the morning."

The water lapped at their feet as they neared their destination.

"You can take a seat while I light the fire." He grabbed a small blanket from the tent, glad he'd had the forethought to snatch it from the hotel room. "You can use this if it gets chilly."

She wrapped it around her shoulders. "Thank you."

"My pleasure."

"If we have sticks, I can get our marshmallows ready and set out the chocolate and graham crackers."

"Right." He fetched the metal roasting sticks he'd picked up from the store. He'd purchased them thinking there was a *gut* chance they wouldn't be able to find any branches on the beach. He'd been correct.

In just a couple of minutes, he had a fire going and Kayla had their goodies out. "I can't remember when I've had this much fun."

He shared a smile with her, loving the way the flames danced in her eyes. "Me, neither."

She handed him a roasting stick and they proceeded to create their midnight snacks. Kayla bit into hers and it took all his restraint not to lean forward and kiss away the chocolate smudge at the edge of her mouth. The joy on her face was priceless.

"How late do you want to stay out here?" She looked sleepy.

"I'd love to watch the sunrise with you, but I'm afraid that might get you into hot water with your folks."

"Yeah, you're probably right."

"You look tired. Do you want to go back?"

"Maybe in a little bit. I'm enjoying this too much."

He bit into his treat and smiled. "Me too."

# EIGHT

Josiah felt a little silly carrying a plate full of food into a hotel lobby. Thankfully, Silas had the presence of mind to suggest covering it with a paper towel. Setting it into a bag would have made his entrance a lot less awkward. Oh well, maybe next time.

His eyes roamed the room in search of Kayla. He spotted her in the dining area piling her own plate with food.

When he called out to her, she turned around and smiled. The excitement on her beautiful face nearly knocked him off his feet. He'd never tire of looking at her.

"You ready?" She approached with a cup in her hand.

"Oh, man. I forgot to grab a drink."

She held up what appeared to be orange juice. "You

can have this if you'd like. We've got bottled water up in the room too."

"I'm happy to have a water." He wouldn't have minded the juice, but he'd rather she drank it since it was what she'd chosen.

He followed her as she led the way to the elevator that he'd dropped her off at the other day.

In a few moments, they were entering the hotel room. "Wow, this is nice."

"Isn't yours?"

"Ours is too, but this is more fancy and much roomier." He eyed the swanky looking bar, complete with barstools, then his gaze meandered to the balcony beyond the sliding glass door. "Do you ever go out there?"

She set her food on the table in the corner, then beckoned him toward the balcony. "Come and see."

The moment they stepped out the sliding glass doors, the gentle coastal breeze caressed his face. He glanced at the chairs on the balcony. "Let's eat out here. Do you want to?"

"That sounds nice. I'll get our food."

An hour later, the breeze became stronger, and they decided to go inside. He'd love to have a balcony to retreat to every day.

"What time are you supposed to meet up with your friends?" Kayla dropped the remainder of their breakfast into the wastebasket.

He drank down the rest of the water in the bottle, smashed it, and then threw it into the trash. "Not till eleven, so I have a couple of hours to spend with you."

He sat on the edge of the high bed and held his hand out to her, then pulled her close. At her full height and him sitting, she stood face to face with him.

"Oh?" Her eyebrow arched upward, and a cute smile danced on her lips. She stared into his eyes and haphazardly caressed the stubble on his cheek, driving him wild in the process.

He captured her mouth with his.

Their lips met again, their kisses growing more intense with each second. Desire surged through his entire being. *Ach*, she was addicting. And in spite of what he'd told Silas, he didn't want to stop. He knew his friend would be disappointed, but at this moment in time, nothing else mattered but Kayla.

His hand glided over her shoulder, then his lips met her skin. "Kayla, I want to..." His lips found hers again and she seemed to melt in his arms. *Ach*, he didn't think he'd ever experienced anything so *wunderbaar*.

She trembled under his touch. "I do too. But I've

never..." Her words trailed off, but he knew what she meant.

His eyes lifted to hers, searching. Because if she wanted to continue down this path, then he definitely wanted to. But he needed to be certain the decision was mutual. "It's my first time too." He admitted.

"It is?" She seemed surprised.

"I promise. I've never loved anyone like this. I've never met anyone like you." It was the truth. He'd never felt this way about *any* girl—Amish or *Englisch*.

The love in her eyes and her passionate response to his advances was all the permission he needed to lift her into his arms and let desire take over.

He shut out the voices in his head telling him this was a bad idea. Silas would just have to be disappointed—if he ever found out. And as of now, Josiah had no plans to share the details of the depth of this romance with his best friend.

Kayla closed her eyes and sighed, loving the feel of Josiah's strong arms around her. She could hardly believe they'd... She swallowed hard.

Looking into Josiah's gaze, she suddenly felt shy. Surely, he was the best thing that had ever happened to her. But...

One thing was for sure, if Mom and Dad were to enter the room with Josiah and her like this, they'd both be in deep trouble. Josiah, if he survived her father's wrath, would likely be in jail. Or the hospital. She frowned at the thought.

No, she wouldn't think about her parents right now. They wouldn't be back until tonight, so they had nothing to worry about.

The only place she wanted her mind to wander was to Josiah and the intimate moments they'd shared. And about their future together. She loved this man with all her heart—with everything in her.

"What are you thinking?" Josiah's husky voice rumbled against her hair, which was likely disheveled.

She turned to him, and he met her lips, his hand gliding down her arm.

He growled. "I don't think I could ever get enough of you."

She giggled at his silliness, and then she sobered.

"I was thinking about us." She pulled back and stared into his eyes. "What are we going to do?"

"Mm. I have some ideas." His lips met her neck.

"I mean, after I leave. I don't want to lose you. Lose us."

"We'll figure something out." He sounded calm and confident, but she wasn't feeling it.

"Will we call each other every week? Every day?"

He frowned. "Call? On the telephone?"

She nodded, smiling at the thought. "And write letters to each other?"

His hand moved over his face, drawing her attention to the attractive dark stubble that had burned her skin earlier. "You can give me your phone number and address."

"And you'll give me yours."

"No."

Her head snapped back. "No? You don't want to give me your phone number and address?"

"No, I can't."

Her narrowing eyes locked on him. "Josiah, you're scaring me. You're not already married or anything, are you?" Her voice screeched. Her heart suddenly stopped beating. What had she gotten herself into?

"No, of course, not! I would never have…" He shook his head, visibly upset that she'd even mentioned that. "I told you it was my first time. I wasn't lying."

She couldn't help it when tears pricked her eyes. "Then why don't you want me to have your phone number?"

"I don't have one."

"You don't have a phone?" She nodded. Did he

believe her to be a fool? "Right. I get it." She shot up from the bed. "And I'm guessing you don't have an address, either. I see how it is. I've been such an idiot."

She frantically began brushing her hair with her fingers because she needed *something* to do.

"Kayla." He sat on the side of the bed and grasped for her hand, but she moved out of reach. "No, that's *not* how it is. You don't understand." His voice sounded desperate.

She tugged her sundress back on. "Then help me to. Because it sounds an awful lot like I just got used."

"I don't really know how to explain it." He held his palms up. "I don't have any privacy. Remember I told you about all my siblings? I don't own my own phone. The phone our family uses isn't in our house. It's a community phone. If you call it, you'd have to leave a message and then other people would hear my message too."

Okay, this sounded weird. But still. "I don't understand how that's a big deal."

"It is to me."

"Why? Because you don't want anyone to know about us? Do you have a girlfriend back in Pennsylvania?" Is that why he looked guilty? "Was this just a summer fling for you, Josiah?"

"No. I promise you; it wasn't. Kayla, I meant those

words I said. I meant all of it. Please, just, can you trust me?"

"I think maybe I've already trusted you with far too much." Her chin trembled.

"Don't do this, Kayla. We only have a couple more days together. I don't want to spend them like this. I don't want you upset with me."

"I don't want us to just leave and forget about each other." She swiped at a tear. "I want *more* than this."

"I know you do." He stepped behind her and slipped his arms around her waist. "I'll call or write to you, okay? I promise." His voice was gentle.

"You better." She turned around and allowed him to pull her close. His hands smoothing her hair and the beating of his heart against her ear calmed the worry in her soul. Like it or not, she'd have to trust him. That was all there was to it.

He lifted her chin. "Look at me."

Her eyes reluctantly met his. They seemed to have this mesmerizing effect on her.

"I love you." He'd said the words with such conviction in his voice that she couldn't help but believe him.

"I love you, too."

# NINE

The remainder of their week had flown by way too fast. They'd spent more time in the water, on the beach, and at the boardwalk, among other things. Kayla hoped Josiah would be true to his word because she had no way to contact him.

He brought her close for a fierce hug and whispered into her hair. "I'm going to miss you like crazy."

She needed to hurry. She'd snuck around the side of the hotel to meet with Josiah. Her parents had already packed up their things and were waiting in the rental car in the hotel parking lot. Their plane was due to leave the airport in just a few hours.

She pulled back and tears pricked her eyes. "I don't want to leave you."

"I know. I don't want you to, either." He thumbed away her tears. "You'll be taking a piece of my heart with you." He leaned down and met her lips, but it ended way too soon.

"Goodbye, Josiah." She needed to go, whether she wanted to or not.

He sucked in a deep breath. "Goodbye, Kayla."

He released her hand, then she jogged around the corner and to the vehicle that would take her away from her sweetheart. She jumped into the backseat and her father began driving. As they exited the parking lot, she spotted Josiah standing near the hotel with his hand raised in farewell.

Her hand pressed against the glass as she attempted to suppress her tears. Surely, this would be the hardest day she'd ever have to face.

The moment Kayla's car disappeared from sight, reality hit him. Josiah knew his life would never be the same again. How could he just go on and live life as it was before they'd met? He couldn't.

He supposed he should be thankful that he and Kayla had met in the first place. She had made this trip a thousand times more special than it would have been without her. But at least he still had his buddies here. They'd take his mind off of missing Kayla. They still had a few days to enjoy the sand and surf before returning home to Pennsylvania.

The thought of returning home didn't appeal to him. He knew before they'd left on this *rumspringa* trip that he'd eventually have to go back, but he wasn't ready yet. Maybe he would be in a few days when it was time to return home.

He patted the pocket that held his wallet with the piece of paper Kayla had written her address and phone number on inside. She was counting on him to contact her, and he couldn't let her down. He sighed. What had he gotten himself into falling in love with a girl that lived all the way across the country?

What did he know about long-distance relationships? He was just an Amish boy from Pennsylvania. Something he'd almost revealed to her when she'd freaked out about him not giving her his address or phone number. But if he had revealed the truth, he suspected she would have freaked out even more. No *Englisch* girl would want to date an Amish boy. His *Englisch* friends had assured him of that.

What to do with himself now... A nice swim in the ocean sounded *gut*.

Josiah's hair appeared damp as he waltzed into his and Silas's hotel room.

"It's about time you showed up. Danny and Allen have been here twice asking if we wanted to go to the boardwalk. I think they finally left without us." Silas frowned. He'd expected to be spending more time with Josiah on this trip, but he'd been absent half the time, it seemed.

"I saw my girl off, then I went for a swim," he confessed.

"Your *Englisch* girl? The reason you've been in la-la land half this trip?"

"Mike was right about the girls."

Silas shrugged. He really didn't want to hear about girls. Especially *Englisch* ones.

"So now that she's gone, you'll be spending more time with your friends?"

"Hey, I've still been spending time with you. We've played volleyball almost every day." Josiah raised a brow. "Do we want to join the guys on the boardwalk then?"

"*Jah*, sure." He eyed his friend. "Are you planning to dry off first?"

Josiah grasped the front of his shirt and pulled it away from his damp skin. "I'm barely wet. By the time we get to the boardwalk I should be completely dry."

"Okay, then. Let's go."

Josiah led the way out the door. "You should go out

for a swim with me later. It was quite invigorating."

"I'd rather rent a boogie board, I think."

"It's a lot of fun, *ain't so*? I'm glad we all learned. Maybe we should try surfing or skimboarding next."

They headed down the hall.

Silas patted his wallet. "Maybe. But my money's running out quick. I think this will be my last trip to the boardwalk."

"I still have some. You can borrow some from me if you want."

They stepped into the elevator, then exited a moment later.

"*Nee*. I don't want to spend more than I budgeted for. Someday I'd like to buy my own place and that will take quite a bit of money." He had dreams that didn't include working in construction with *Dat*, but he'd need to work with *Dat* long enough for him to save up for it. It wasn't easy since he was only allowed to keep half the money he earned, but he was thankful for that little bit, at least.

Josiah grinned, as they headed out of their hotel and down the street. "*Jah*, me too. Someday."

"Can you believe we only have three more days? It went by way too fast, ain't not?"

When screams echoed through the air, Silas lifted his eyes toward the amusement park. Excitement surged at the thought of going on the rides again.

"Let's make the most of it. I'm going on that rollercoaster again!" Josiah's grin filled his entire face.

"Me too. And I want more of that taffy."

# TEN

Silas yawned and sat up as light filtered through the hotel window. It had been strange not having to go out to work day after day. He had a feeling he might be out of practice when he returned home. He'd cherish these days the rest of his life because they would likely never happen again.

"Hey, Joe. Do you want to—" He glanced over at Josiah's vacant bed and frowned.

Silas listened closely but the shower didn't sound like it was running. He sprung from the bed, then noticed a slip of paper with the hotel emblem on the top sitting on the nightstand between the two queen beds.

He picked up the note and read the words.

*Silas, I went for an early morning swim. See you at breakfast. Joe.*

Silas glanced at the small alarm clock near the bed.

It was only seven thirty. They usually headed to the dining area around eight. Josiah should be back soon.

He made himself a cup of coffee, then strolled to the window and took in the beautiful view. The only appropriate word he could find for the ocean was breathtaking. He supposed it could be called amazing or wonderful or even magnificent. But none of those words seemed adequate.

His eyes scanned the beach. Maybe he could spot Josiah on his way back to the hotel. Or maybe not.

He stripped off his night clothes and quickly dressed in the *Englisch* clothes Josiah had insisted he purchase. It still felt awkward wearing them. A part of him looked forward to going back home and things returning to normal. Because as much as he'd been enjoying himself on this *rumspringa* trip, there was still no place like home. There was something to be said for familiarity.

Silas and Joe and their families had a busy harvest ahead of them. He looked forward to fall, when the Beachys would host their annual harvest party, including their famed corn maze. It wasn't something they invited the public to—just an end of the season celebration with their immediate Amish community. But each year, they had a wonderful *gut* time, spending an evening together and indulging in delicious food, fun, and games.

A knock on the door reminded him that Josiah probably hadn't taken his hotel key with him. A good idea if he was swimming in the ocean.

Silas pulled the door open, but Danny and Allen stood in the opening instead. "I thought you were Josiah."

"*Nee.* We came to see if you guys are ready to go down to breakfast." Allen peeked over his shoulder.

"I am, but Joe's not back yet." Silas grimaced.

"Where did he go?" Danny asked.

Silas pointed to the end table. "He left a note saying he was going out for a swim this morning. Said he'd see me at breakfast."

Allen shrugged. "He's probably already in the dining room, then."

"*Jah*, maybe," Silas agreed.

"Let's go then?"

"Okay. I can definitely eat."

"Hm...I don't see Josiah anywhere. Do you?" Danny raised a brow, and Allen and Silas both shook their heads.

Silas frowned, surveying the dining area. "Should we be worried? I'm not sure what time he headed out there, but I was up at seven thirty and he was already gone."

"It's been almost two hours." Allen's lips twisted.

"I think we should go look for him if he isn't back in the room when I return." The truth was, Silas was beginning to worry. Who went out swimming for over two hours?

Silas glanced down at his plateful of food. All of a sudden, it didn't look so *gut*.

"You don't want to wait?" Danny tossed his empty plate into the trash can, then grabbed another piece of fruit. "Maybe he met another girl."

"*Nee*, I don't think so." Silas didn't have a *gut* feeling about this. His eyes meandered to the ocean through the window in the dining area. Not that he'd be able to see anything from this distance.

"We can check the beach and maybe walk the boardwalk and look in the shops." Allen suggested. "I don't know where else he'd be."

"The girl he was spending time with left already, ain't so?" Danny bit into an apple.

How could Danny eat at a time like this? Silas had lost his appetite. He had a feeling it wouldn't return until their friend was found safe and sound. Maybe he was just overreacting. "Joe said she left yesterday morning. She was flying on an airplane to the other side of the country, was what he said."

Allen dug into his second plate of waffles. "Well, if

he didn't go swimming, where would he have gone?"

"He wouldn't have left a note saying he was going for a swim if he wasn't." Silas insisted. He knew Josiah better than just about anybody, and Josiah didn't make a habit out of lying. If he said he was going swimming, then that was what he did.

Unless something had happened to him. But Silas didn't want to go there. Not now.

Silas tapped his fingers on the table. "Are you two done yet?"

"You should eat something, Silas. Don't worry about Josiah. I'm sure he's fine." At least Allen seemed confident.

"I think I'm going to go back to our room, then take a walk on the beach if Joe isn't back yet." Because just sitting around wasn't an option.

"Wait." Danny stood from the table. "We should come up with a plan. Let's all search, then we can meet back up at, say, eleven o'clock? That should give us enough time to check all the places out where we think he may have gone."

"He could have decided to check out one of the restaurants." Allen noted.

"By himself?" That seemed like a stretch.

"Listen, Silas. There's a *gut* chance he's already back at the room."

"*Jah*, I hope you're right."

After two hours of searching the beach, Josiah still hadn't been located. All three of them had searched the beach and water for the first hour, then Allen and Danny headed for the boardwalk.

Silas lifted the binoculars to his eyes again, scanning the water. "Where are you, Josiah?" He said under his breath.

*Gott, please help us find him or let him show up soon.*

"Looking for something?"

Silas turned toward the male voice. A lifeguard, clad in red shorts, stood behind him. This morning when he'd looked out his hotel window, he hadn't seen any lifeguards on duty. Which meant, no one would have been there to rescue Josiah if he had trouble in the water.

"My friend. He left a note saying he was going out swimming this morning."

"This morning? What time?" Concern laced the young man's voice. Silas guessed him to be around his own age or maybe a year or two older.

"I'm not sure. When I woke up at seven thirty, his note was on the table."

The young man glanced at his watch and frowned. "And you haven't heard from him at all?"

"No. He was supposed to meet us for breakfast and never showed up. That's why my friends and I have been out here looking for him. They headed to the boardwalk to see if maybe he'd gone there." Silas sighed. He was quite certain that Josiah would not have gone to the boardwalk by himself.

"Will you come back to the lifeguard station with me? I'm going to call in some help."

Silas nodded. Help would be welcome. "Sure."

*Please,* Gott. *I don't want to return home without Josiah.*

The remainder of the day had been fraught with activity—interviews with police officers, probes by teams of search and rescue workers, helicopters flying overhead along the beach and water, and Coast Guard boats out in the ocean—all in search of his missing best friend. With each minute that passed, despair set in deeper.

Once the sun had gone down, the rescuers didn't seem hopeful that Josiah would be found. All searches had proven fruitless. The last time Josiah had been seen alive and well was in the hotel's video footage.

He'd exited the hotel and headed for the beach until he was out of view of the camera. Then he seemed to have disappeared without a trace.

Everything Josiah had brought with him was still in the hotel room. His clothes, his belongings, his wallet with his money inside, his hotel key card. Everything.

The only thing Silas could come up with was that his best friend was now gone forever. He hadn't wanted to admit it to himself. But after searching all day, he was weary, and most of his hope for finding his friend had evaporated with the ocean's mist.

Silas now stared out his hotel window at the darkness that had descended. Darkness. It was all he felt now.

Like it or not, he was going to have to call Alvin and Ada Beachy and let them know what was going on. Maybe he should have called them already, but he'd put it off for as long as possible in hopes that Josiah would be found safe and sound.

But that hadn't been the case.

A part of him wished that Josiah would have somehow already returned home. That wasn't likely, of course, but he hoped for it, nonetheless.

He'd been holding it together pretty well, but the moment he picked up the telephone to call Josiah's folks, grief grasped ahold of his heart and he broke down. It had taken him a half hour before he was able to make the call. The weight of reality sat heavy on his chest.

His best friend was gone, and the thought of returning home without him seemed impossible.

*"Why,* Gott?" He cried. *"Why did You take him away from us?"*

He knew that questioning *Der Herr* wasn't the Amish way. He was expected to just accept it as *Gott's* will and move on. *Nee,* he wasn't going to do that.

He needed a drink.

Silas pounded on Danny and Allen's door to the room across the hallway.

The door swung open. "Silas? Did something happen? Did they find Josiah?"

"*Nee.* I need a drink."

Danny glanced at Allen, who handed him a bottle of water.

"*Nee,* not that."

"We still have some soda." Allen frowned.

Without a word, Silas brushed past them and dug into the icebox. He pulled out a brown bottle.

"Silas." Danny and Allen shared a look. "You don't drink."

He chugged the entire bottle, set it on the table, then reached for another one. "I do now."

"Give me your keys." Silas demanded.

"My keys?" Allen's forehead creased and his hand slid over his shirt pocket. "What for?"

"I need to get out of here."

"No, Silas. You're not driving right now." Danny insisted. "Not like this."

"I need to...I have to..." Tears burned his eyes. "I can't do this. I can't stay here."

"Then we can go home. I'm sure the police probably have all they need from us."

Silas thought of being at home without Josiah there. No running next door to his house and the two of them going for a walk or a buggy ride. No more talks about work and *maed* and stuff. He'd never get to do those things with Josiah again. He'd never see his friend again.

"Silas? We'll leave tomorrow morning, okay?" Allen assured. "If the police are fine with it."

"You can crash here with us if you'd like. We'll all feel better after a *gut* night's sleep."

Danny's words had been meant to comfort, but did he realize how stupid they sounded to Silas's ears?

No amount of sleep would make him feel better. No amount of sleep would bring Josiah back. He was unsure if he could even sleep in the first place. How *could* he sleep when Josiah was lost in the middle of the ocean?

"I can't go home! We can't leave without him." Silas shot out of the room, not caring what the guys would think. What did it even matter anymore? He wouldn't drive anywhere, but he could run as far as his legs would carry him. That would have to be enough for now.

Several hours later, he woke up on the beach, not even bothering to brush the sand off his face. He stared out at the vast watery graveyard that had stolen his best friend, and he cursed it.

Funny how the ocean no longer brought calm. Now, the only thing he felt was sorrow and despair. He'd never see his best friend again. No matter how long he sat on this beach, his life would never be the same. His heart would never be the same. It was as if a part of him had been cut off and was now missing. A piece of him was out in the ocean, and he was no longer whole.

Nor would he ever be again.

# ELEVEN

Kayla had checked the answering machine the moment they'd arrived home. Not that she'd expected Josiah to call right away. She couldn't help but hope he would, though.

The mailbox had been absent of correspondence from Josiah too, although she knew it was too soon for a letter to have arrived.

She continued to check it faithfully every day, just in case. Because someday there *would* be either a letter or a phone call. She was sure of it. Josiah had said he loved her, and she believed him. Maybe she should have asked him *when* exactly he planned to contact her.

She sighed, then continued to her room. At least she had their photo strip. She'd already gazed at it a hundred times. She would never get tired of Josiah's smile. Or of the love and excitement and joy in his eyes. The photos summed up their time together so perfectly.

He'd been shocked when she kissed him for the first time. He hadn't been expecting it while they were in the middle of their photographic adventure. She initiated it, but he'd quickly taken over. And, boy, could he kiss!

She'd dreamed of his lips on hers many times since they'd said goodbye. Had he done the same? Was he thinking of her now?

"Kayla!" It was Mom.

Time to help with dinner. "Coming!"

She smiled at the photos one more time, gave her favorite picture of Josiah a quick kiss, then headed to the kitchen.

She hadn't mentioned Josiah to Mom yet. Maybe she would someday, but now she wanted to keep the memories to herself. She cherished the secret moments they'd spent together and keeping them inside her heart felt special, somehow.

Had Josiah shared their romance with his friends? She was certain they knew about her, but did Josiah divulge any details? A part of her hoped he wouldn't.

"I can tell someone has had a lot on their mind lately." Mom handed her the bowl of tossed salad and she placed it on the table.

Kayla retrieved plates and forks for the meal and set them on the table as well. She smiled. "Yeah."

"Want to talk about it?"

She shrugged. "I met someone."

Mom's eyebrows lifted. "Oh? On our trip?"

"Yeah." She really wanted to show Mom the photos, but she wasn't sure how she'd react to the one where her and Josiah were kissing.

"That's nice, honey. I hope you had a good time. Your father and I were so busy, but we had some fun too." Mom sliced the french bread that would go with the lasagna. "Did you go on any rides with this boy?"

"Yes. The rollercoaster, the Ferris wheel, the bumper cars." She shrugged and laughed. "A lot of them."

"Will you call your dad to the table? It's all ready."

"Sure, Mom." She skipped out to the garage. "Daddy, Mom said dinner's ready."

He slid out from under the old car he'd been working on. He called it his baby because he'd owned it since high school. Sometimes, they'd drive the classic to car shows and fifties diners. It had always been a fun thing to do with her parents. One time, she'd even won a hula hoop contest.

"What's on the menu tonight?" Dad asked.

"Mom made lasagna." Kayla led the way inside.

He sniffed the air as he entered the house. "Smells delicious, hon."

"I hope it is. I tried out a new recipe." Mom's voice echoed from the other room.

When they stepped into the kitchen, Mom eyed Dad's grease-darkened hands. "Did you wash up?"

He glanced at his hands and laughed. "I did, actually."

"Let's eat then," Mom took her usual seat, then handed a dish to Dad.

Kayla automatically thought of the breakfast she and Josiah had shared on the hotel balcony and smiled. "How come we don't pray before our meals?" She blurted out.

Dad's fork poised in mid-air, and he and Mom shared a look.

"We're not religious, honey. You know that." Mom blinked.

"I know, but why?" She was genuinely curious. She'd never even really thought much about it until now.

"That's just not the way we were raised." Dad sipped his tea. "Why are you asking about this all of a sudden?"

"Oh, I don't know." She shrugged. "I just noticed that some people pray before they eat. I thought it was interesting."

Was Josiah religious? She guessed he probably was, since he prayed before his meals. What would a future with a religious person look like? She wondered.

"This dinner is exquisite, honey." Dad changed the subject, then looked at Kayla. "Are you excited about school starting tomorrow, pumpkin?"

She'd always loved Dad's nickname for her. "It's just orientation, I think."

"And then you start on Tuesday?"

"I think so. I'm anxious to talk to Sierra. She and her parents were going to tour some college campuses." The Italian flavors mingled on Kayla's tongue.

"That's right. It's her last year." Mom chimed in.

Kayla sipped her water. "I'll miss her next year."

"Yeah, but you'll be there before you know it. Enjoy it while it lasts, because once it's over, it's gone forever. All you'll have is your memories."

She wondered about Josiah. They hadn't talked much about school, only that he worked on a farm with his father. She wondered now if he had any ambitions of going to college. Had he wanted to become a farmer like his dad?

She smiled, thinking of herself as a farmer's wife. What on earth would she do on a farm all day? What did farmer's wives even do? Maybe it was something she should look up.

"What are you smiling about, honey?" Mom asked.

"Ah, nothing. Just my future, I guess." She studied her parents. They were both successful businesspeople.

"Do you still want to go to that travel school?"

She'd always thought she wanted to be a flight attendant, but now she wasn't so sure. Of course, if she traveled, she'd be able to visit Pennsylvania on the airline's dime. "I'm not sure what I want to do yet."

"Well, there's no hurry to figure things out. You still have two years of high school. And then, if you decide to go to a junior college, you can just take general education courses. Most of those will transfer to a university. That's what I did." Mom began clearing the table.

Kayla popped up to help. "I'll do dishes, Mom."

Mom's eyes flew wide. "Did I hear right? Is Kayla volunteering to do the dishes?"

Her parents stared at each other for a moment.

"Yes, that's what I said." Because if she might someday become a farmer's wife, she imagined she'd be washing the dishes. "I want to learn how to cook, too. Especially your pot pie." She had a feeling a farmer would like pot pie.

Dad about fell out of his chair. "Who are you, and what have you done with my daughter?"

Kayla just laughed off his comment.

Mom moved close to Dad and massaged his shoulders. "I think our little girl might be growing up."

Kayla nibbled the inside of her lip. They had no idea.

# TWELVE

Silas had thought there was no place like home. Yet, home was no longer the same.

It killed him to face everybody—especially Josiah's family. Somehow, he felt like he'd failed them. Why should *he* get to come home alive and well? Why did *he* survive and Josiah not? He wished it would have been him instead. Josiah didn't deserve this. His family didn't deserve this.

He felt like he'd asked *Gott* why a thousand times. And a thousand times, there'd been no answer.

"It was *Gott's* will." Everybody said it, but was it really true? Why would *Der Herr* will his best friend's death? It didn't make sense, to his thinking.

"Silas?" A knock on the door accompanied his brother Paul's voice.

"*Kumm* in."

His brother sat on the edge of the bed next to him

and released a sigh. Paul's hand clasped Silas's shoulder. "I'm sorry about Josiah."

Silas shoved away a frustrated tear and nodded to acknowledge his brother. "He was my best friend. I'll never forget him."

Paul's eyes clouded over, and he moved closer. He touched his brother's forearm and locked eyes with him. "If you want, I can be your new best friend."

His brother's heartfelt words touched him deeply. A heavy sob escaped his chest and he grabbed onto his brother and held on for dear life. He truly had the best family.

Silas regained his composure. "I'd like that, Paul."

*Jah*, he'd lost Josiah and it hurt like crazy. But there were still blessings all around him. He shouldn't forget that.

*Mamm* appeared at the opening of his door. "*Buwe, kumm* into the kitchen. Your *dat* and I want to discuss something with all of you *kinner*."

Silas glanced at Paul and they both rose and followed *Mamm*. *Dat* sat at his usual place at the kitchen table. "Sit, *buwe*."

Martha, Susan, and Nathaniel were seated too, but Silas guessed that baby Emily was probably in bed already.

"You're probably wondering why we've called you here."

"*Jah*, especially since there's no food." Paul deadpanned.

Silas elbowed Paul for his comment. "This isn't the time for jokes."

"*Nee*, it isn't, but we all need to smile sometimes." *Mamm* reminded.

How long had it been since he'd smiled? Two weeks, at least? He was quite certain he hadn't smiled since Josiah's disappearance. It seemed like it happened forever ago, yet it seemed like *chust* yesterday. How could that be?

"This is going to seem sudden. Especially to you, Silas." *Dat*'s words were sober.

Silas frowned. What were they talking about?

"We spoke with the bishop, and he believes this will be a *gut* thing for our family."

"*What* would be a *gut* thing?" He wished they'd *chust* come out and say it.

"Patience, *sohn*." *Mamm* reprimanded.

"There is an Amish sister church in Indiana." *Dat* explained. "We will sell our place and move. The land is much more affordable there, so we believe that will help you *buwe* when it's time to take a *fraa* and start your own families. We can buy property twice the size of what we have now. There is a place for sale right now. It already has a *dawdi haus* attached."

"But we don't need a *dawdi haus*. Our *grosseldern* already have homes with *Onkel* Marvin and *Aenti* Reba." Silas protested. This was a terrible idea.

"We're looking toward the future, *sohn*."

Right. The future. Something Josiah no longer had. It made Silas wonder how many days *he* had left.

"But we'll have to leave our friends." Martha's voice sounded distraught.

"She's talking about Jaden Beachy, her *schatzi*." Paul teased.

"He is not, Paul!" Martha insisted. "We're *chust* friends at school."

Silas frowned at his brother. "Paul, *nee*. Leave Martha alone."

He hadn't realized his *schweschder* was friends with Josiah's younger *bruder*, but it made sense because they were in school together. He thought on it for a moment, and that was when he remembered Josiah mentioning his younger *bruder* Jaden had taken a liking to Martha.

"That's one of the reasons we want to leave soon. Before the *kinner* start up school again. It would be *gut* if we have a chance to meet some of the families in the *g'may* first."

"Is this already settled?" That was all he needed to know.

"This is what your *mamm* and I have decided, *jah*." *Dat* rubbed his beard. "We thought moving before any of you find someone to get hitched to was probably a *gut* time. And since Josiah is gone, we feel the move will be easier for you now."

Nothing was easy now. Didn't they understand that?

"A change of scenery will do us all *gut*." *Mamm* nodded.

So, that was it. They were transplanting to Indiana.

"When will we move?" Paul asked.

"We will begin packing tomorrow and move after the weekend. That will give us all one last time to say goodbye to the *g'may*."

Tears shimmered in Martha's eyes, then she vacated her chair and bolted from the room.

"Told you," Paul said.

*Mamm* sighed and rose from her seat. "I will go talk to her."

"This will be a *gut* thing. You will see." *Dat* nodded. "You may be excused for bed now."

# THIRTEEN

Books in arms, Kayla and her friend Sierra strolled down the school's corridor heading to their mutual first period class. Fortunately, they had extra time to gab this morning.

Kayla turned to Sierra. "You still haven't told me about your trip. Did you figure out which college you want to go to?"

Sierra nodded. "I think so. I'm leaning toward Cuesta, then Cal Poly."

"Because they're at the beach, right?" Kayla grinned, knowing her friend. "That's so cool."

"Yes, and I liked the campuses too." Sierra opened her locker and switched out her books. "You'll have to come visit me next year."

"I will." Kayla shrugged. "But I have a feeling you'll be off making new college friends. You'll probably forget all about me."

"I will not." Sierra's eyebrow arched. "Now, tell me all about Ocean City."

"I still can't believe we haven't talked about this yet."

"I know, right?"

"A met someone." Kayla bounced on her toes.

"What? *Someone*, as in a *boyfriend*?"

Kayla nodded enthusiastically.

"All the way in Maryland?"

"New Jersey."

"I thought Ocean City was in Maryland."

"There's one there too. I went to the one in New Jersey. It was closest to my dad's meetings."

"So, he's from New Jersey? What's his name?"

"No, he's from Pennsylvania. His name is Josiah Beachy." She pulled out the photo strip they'd taken at the boardwalk. She'd been aching to share this with Sierra, but they'd both been so busy. "Isn't he cute?"

Sierra's eyes nearly exploded. "No way! Oh, my word, Kayla! He's gorgeous!" Sierra squealed.

"I know, right?" Happiness filled her every time she looked at their pictures.

Sierra gestured toward the photos. "And you obviously kissed him."

"Mm hm." She giggled.

"So, tell me all about him." Sierra practically sang the words.

"He's a farmer."

"A farmer?" Sierra laughed, glanced at the pictures, then shrugged. "I guess he could pass for a farm boy."

"Well, he said he works on his dad's farm. I don't know if he plans to have his own farm. He didn't say."

"Interesting. How long did you two spend together?"

"Well, my parents were gone most of the time, so we spent time together every day. But he was there with his friends, so we weren't together *all* the time."

"What did you do?"

"Everything, pretty much."

"Wait." Sierra scrutinized her. "What do you mean by *everything*?"

Kayla's heart pounded. She hadn't planned on telling Sierra about *that*.

"You know. We went to the boardwalk, rode the rides together, went boogie boarding, all that." She couldn't wipe the smile off her face. It was so fun to share her adventures with someone who understood.

"I am *so* jealous of you right now." Sierra stared at the photos. "Wow, he is so hot!"

"I know, right? And he's a total sweetheart, too. He even set up a tent on the beach at night and we went for a walk and then roasted marshmallows."

"That is the ultimate summer romance right there." Sierra rolled her eyes. "And I declined your invitation to go with you so I could visit colleges. Worst mistake ever."

"I think your parents had some say so in that, right?"

"But still." Sierra shook her head. "So, have you talked to him since you've been back?"

"No, not yet. He said he would call or write."

"And he hasn't yet?" Sierra's lips turned down.

"Well, it hasn't been *that* long, really." At least, that was what she'd been telling herself. "Two weeks."

"If he doesn't contact you soon, you should just call him then. I mean, what if he like lost your phone number or something?"

Kayla frowned. That would be the worst thing ever. "I don't have his phone number. He said he didn't have a phone."

Sierra's skeptical eyes zoned in on Kayla. "Who in this day and age doesn't own a phone?"

"I think his family might be really old fashioned or something, because he has a ton of siblings. So, I guess I'm not that surprised by the phone anymore, now that I think about it."

"That's kind of weird, isn't it?" Sierra's lips twisted.

"It is, but people live different back there, I guess." Kayla shrugged.

"Well, if he's old fashioned maybe he'd be more comfortable if you just write him a letter."

Right. But she didn't have his address, either. If Josiah had in mind to desert her, it would be quite convenient for him to do so. She really should have pushed for some type of contact information from him. She was kicking herself for it now.

Kayla sighed. *Josiah, you better contact me.*

"We're going to the game Friday, right?"

Kayla grinned. High school football games were one of their favorite things to do. "You said you wanted to go to all of them this year."

"I do. After I graduate, they will be a thing of the past. We need to make this year count."

Sierra and Kayla entered the classroom, but they were the only students present so far. They slid into their normal spots, next to each other. Kayla had been thankful they'd been allowed to choose their seats at the beginning of the semester.

"I'll miss you next year."

"I'm not worried about you. You'll find some senior guy and won't think about me one bit."

Kayla frowned. "I don't plan on dating anyone. I'm holding out for Josiah."

"Wow, he really did affect you, didn't he?" Sierra's forehead wrinkled. "So, do you think you might marry this Pennsylvania guy?"

"I don't know. I hope so. Eventually, maybe. But I have to finish high school first, obviously." Kayla glanced up as some of their classmates began trickling in.

"Where does he go to school?"

"He doesn't. He's nineteen, so he would have graduated last year, probably." They hadn't talked much about school. "He didn't mention college, so I assumed he didn't plan to go."

"Well, you said he was working on the farm, right? I wonder if farming makes much money." Sierra had always been fascinated by occupations that earned a lot of money.

Kayla, not so much. As far as she was concerned, Josiah Beachy could be dirt poor and she'd still love him. "I'm sure it does for some. Look at Tara Anderson. Her parents are farmers and she's one of the most well-off in the whole school."

"What kind of car does he drive?"

"I have no idea. I didn't ask."

"What? Didn't you guys drive anywhere?"

"No, everything was within walking distance. Besides, he was there with his friends. I don't even know whose car they drove."

"Were his friends cute, too?"

Kayla's lips twisted. "I don't know. I didn't meet them."

"Why not?"

"I don't know. He mentioned it, but I guess we just never got around to it."

"That's weird. Maybe he thought his friends would hit on you."

"I don't know."

At that moment, the bell rang and the teacher cut off their conversation. Kayla glanced down at her photo strip one more time and slipped it into her bag, certain she would cherish the photos forever.

# FOURTEEN

Today was the day.

The Miller family would embark on a journey that would change all their lives. *Dat* had said it was for the better. Silas wasn't so sure.

One thing about having Josiah as a best friend was that he'd always been more outgoing than Silas. And that meant going to new places was a lot less daunting. Silas didn't feel like attending a young folks' gathering in a new Amish district where he knew no one.

Being friends with Josiah had been easy. They had been close in age. They lived next door to each other. They attended the same church. They'd gone to the same school.

This would be different, for sure. He understood Martha's reluctance. Paul, on the other hand, seemed eager to meet new people and explore new places. Too bad his *bruder* wasn't closer in age to him. By the time

Paul started going with the young folks', Silas would likely be hitched and maybe even have his own place.

Which made him think. Now that Josiah wasn't around, maybe he should consider a special friendship with a *maedel*. Just maybe a *fraa* would help heal his heart. But was he even ready for that kind of relationship? Was he ready to put his single days behind him?

*Ach*, he was only nineteen, but he felt so much older now. Like losing Josiah had drained some of the life out of him. Had it? He supposed grief could do that to a body.

"I think we've got everything all packed up and ready to go." *Dat* said, glancing at the van and trailer they'd rented. Their *Englisch* driver had just been waiting for them to say the word.

Tears gathered in Silas's eyes as he embraced Alvin and Ada Beachy. Josiah's folks had come to see them off.

"*Denki* for being a friend to Josiah. We couldn't have asked *Der Herr* for a better one for him," Alvin said.

"We will see him again someday, *ain't not*?" Silas had said the words, but he wondered in his heart if they were true. Josiah hadn't been baptized yet. He'd died outside the Amish church.

"We will hope for that. Only *Der Herr* knows." Sadness shimmered in both Alvin's and Ada's eyes. Did they feel Josiah was lost forever?

Silas prayed it wasn't so. He didn't want to think that his best friend might not be in Heaven.

"*Kumm* back and visit us sometime. You will always be welcome." Ada insisted.

He swallowed hard. Returning here would be difficult, for sure. "*Denki*. I might do that someday."

Silas knew he'd never forget the image of Josiah's folks waving goodbye. If only he'd had a chance to say goodbye to his friend.

"Kayla, where have you been? Have you been sick this whole week?"

Like a dog. It was Friday already, and this was the first day she'd been in school this week. "Yeah, pretty much. Mom thinks it was the stomach flu."

"Did you go to the doctor? What did they say?"

"No. I haven't gone to the doctor. You know I hate going." She already knew she was sick, and she already had medicine at home. Why did she need a doctor to tell her what she already knew? She didn't see the point.

"Well, because you haven't been here, I had to deal

with Cecilia Maxwell. Mr. Bradshaw paired us up for lab. Ugh, she drives me crazy."

"Oh, no." Kayla shoved her notebook in Sierra's arms and made a mad dash for the girls' bathroom. Fortunately, they were located close by. She barely made it before losing her breakfast.

She heard footsteps entering the bathroom. "Kayla, what's wrong with you?"

"I'm not even sure." It was a good thing she'd thought to bring her toothbrush to school.

"Kayla, are you—oh no." Sierra covered her mouth and her eyes bulged. "Kayla." She yanked her close and whispered in her ear, although Kayla was pretty sure they were the only girls in the restroom. "Did you sleep with Josiah?"

Kayla chirped, "Sleep?"

Sierra's eyes narrowed. "Don't act all innocent. You *know* what I mean."

Kayla admitted to it with a nod.

"Just once?"

Kayla shook her head. "A few times." She swallowed.

"I bet you're pregnant."

She shook her head. "No, I can't be." Kayla's chin began to wobble as Sierra's words registered.

Sierra tugged on her arm. "Let's go see the nurse.

I'm pretty sure they have pregnancy tests in the nurse's office."

"No! I can't go see the nurse. They'll tell my parents!" She shoved away a stupid tear.

"No, they won't. Trust me."

"I'm not seeing the nurse." She jammed her arms across her chest.

"Okay, fine." Sierra sighed. "But we're going to the store and buying you a test at lunchtime. Unless you don't think you'll make it till lunch."

"No, let's go now. I need to know."

"Have you heard from him at all? Has he called you yet?"

Tears surfaced again. "No! And I don't think he's going to."

"Shh." Sierra touched her shoulder. "He still might. It's only been, what? A month, right? Maybe he's just busy on his farm."

Kayla knew Sierra was only trying to make her feel better, but it wasn't working. With everything in her, she hoped Sierra was wrong. It couldn't be a baby. Maybe a disease or some sickness or *something*. Anything but Josiah's baby.

Thirty minutes later, Kayla's fingers trembled as she held a positive pregnancy test in her hands. She slid to the floor in Sierra's private bathroom. Her friend's parents both worked away from home, so it had been the perfect place to escape to.

"Is it positive?" Sierra's voice called through the door.

Kayla sobbed, unable to bring herself to speak.

Sierra let herself in, then took the pregnancy test from Kayla's hand, and placed it on the bathroom counter. Then she joined Kayla on the floor and slung her arm around her friend's shoulders. "It's okay. It's going to be all right. You'll see."

"What am I going to do?" she cried. "I can't tell my parents. My dad's going to kill me."

"No, he won't. He'll be upset. But you know it won't be the first time. Remember that time we were out late and your dad came looking for us?" Sierra rubbed Kayla's arm. "I know your parents. They won't kick you out or anything."

"Sierra, I can't." An avalanche of tears fell. "He said he loved me! Why hasn't he contacted me? I don't understand."

"Maybe he's not who you thought he was."

"He said it was his first time." Kayla didn't want to admit it, but Sierra was probably right. "I was so stupid to believe him. How could I be so gullible?"

"Because you loved him, honey. We don't always think straight when we're in love." Sierra handed her a wad of tissues.

"I don't know how I'm going to tell my parents." Kayla dabbed her eyes.

Sierra held her hand. "Do you want me to come with you?"

"Would you?" She sniffled.

"Yes. That's what friends are for." Sierra squeezed her hand.

Gratefulness filled Kayla's heart. No, Josiah wasn't here to share the responsibility. But having her friend by her side would help her deal with the tumultuous days ahead.

If only Josiah would just write a letter or call. A postcard, even. *Anything.* Anything to let her know that he'd cared for her, that their love hadn't been one-sided. Anything to let her know that she wasn't alone.

Sierra joined Kayla's family for dinner that night. Now that the meal was over and dishes had been washed, Kayla attempted to summon the courage to say what needed to be said. The two of them joined her parents in the den.

"Mom, Dad, I have something I need to say." Kayla blew out a breath, in hopes of calming her pounding heart.

Dad set his newspaper aside and Mom dropped her crossword puzzle book in her lap.

"First of all, I want to warn you. You're not going to like what I have to say. Will you promise not to get too upset?"

Her parents' gazes bounced back and forth between Kayla and Sierra.

"What are you two up to?" Dad frowned.

"Sierra doesn't have anything to do with this." At least her parents were sitting down. "Mom, Dad..."

Her chin trembled and Sierra squeezed her hand. "Just tell them," Sierra whispered.

"Tell us what?" Mom's brow lowered.

"I'm pregnant." She squeaked out the words.

"You're what?!" Dad jumped up. She knew he'd be upset.

"Kayla, why?" Mom's voice sounded sad, sympathetic.

"You are barely sixteen, Kayla! You cannot be pregnant," her father insisted. "Whose is it?"

"His name is Josiah."

Dad picked up the telephone. "Well, you're going to call him right now. And he's going to haul his hide down here and face us like a man."

"I don't have his phone number." Kayla swallowed.

"She met him in Ocean City." Sierra volunteered.

"Ocean City?" Both of her parents said it at the same time.

"I knew we never should have left her alone." Mom insisted.

"Did he force you?" Dad's distraught look and clenched hands made Kayla think he was ready to pound someone into the ground.

"No. We fell in love." Kayla couldn't stop a tear from streaming down her cheek.

"He needs to come and marry you, then." Dad visibly began to relax.

"He doesn't know about the baby. I don't have any way to get ahold of him."

"Oh, we're going to find him, alright." Dad was adamant. If only it were possible. Because if Josiah knew he had a baby on the way, maybe he *would* come to California and marry her. "Where does he live?"

"Pennsylvania." At least she knew that much. "But I already tried to find him on the computer. The only Josiah Beachy I found in Pennsylvania lived in the 1800s."

"The 1800s?" Mom shook her head. "There has to be more Josiah Beachys."

"Unless he was lying to her about his name." Sierra spoke up.

Kayla's mouth hung open. She hadn't even thought

of that. She closed her eyes and forbade the tears that threatened.

"I'm sorry. But if he didn't give you a way to contact him, there's a good chance he wasn't truthful about other things too." Sierra frowned. "Let's face it. This guy is just a jerk. You might be better off without him."

Kayla had been trying not to think of him that way. She'd been wanting to give him the benefit of the doubt. But Sierra was probably right.

All Josiah Beachy, if that was even his name, had been looking for was a good time. And apparently, he knew the exact words to say to get her to play along. Except she hadn't been playing.

Why in the world had she gone and fallen in love with Josiah Beachy?

# FIFTEEN

"We're almost there." The *Englisch* driver turned onto a road.

They passed a couple of houses that looked like they could belong to Amish folks. Barns and silos stood proud. Laundry fluttered on clotheslines. But it was so different than Pennsylvania.

Weren't the Amish houses required to be white in this district? Apparently not.

"One of the families lives there." *Dat* pointed to a two-story tan farmhouse.

Silas eyed the large greenhouses on the property. At least he knew where they'd be getting their produce until they could grow their own.

A young boy waved as they drove past.

"He might be Nathaniel's age." *Mamm* remarked.

They continued down the country road as it dipped and rose, and Silas almost became carsick.

How would Strider make it up and down these hills with the buggy? Was this road even safe for an Amish buggy? It seemed not.

The driver turned off onto an even narrower road, then turned into a driveway.

"This is it." *Dat* pointed out the window, a slight grin lifting.

A large barn and a couple of small outbuildings sat about a hundred feet off the right side of the driveway. Directly across was their new house, which was white, to Silas's approval. It had a decent size front porch that begged for a swing. Just by looking at the structure, Silas guessed the smaller room attached to the right of the main dwelling was the *dawdi haus*.

"Looks like it needs some work," Paul said.

"It'll keep us all busy for a while." *Mamm* agreed.

Silas had wondered if it had been a *gut* idea purchasing the property sight unseen, but it didn't look too bad.

"We knew it would. But it's nothing we can't handle." *Dat* opened the door as the van rolled to a stop. "The other trailer should arrive later today. The driver assured me he'd be taking *gut* care of the horses."

No doubt, he'd have to calm Strider down after the drive. Silas joined his father outside, and the rest of the family tumbled out of the van as well.

"I'm *chust* glad we have an inside bathroom," Susan chirped, quickly following *Mamm* inside the house. She'd been complaining about needing to use the restroom for the last twenty minutes. Since they'd been so close, *Dat* hadn't wanted to stop in the small town nearby.

"*Buwe*, let's unload the trailer so Dex can be on his way." *Dat* called them all over. "Your *Mamm* and *schweschdern* will take care of things in the house."

"I guess we'll have to wait to see the inside." Paul sighed.

"It isn't going anywhere." *Dat* chuckled. "You'll be seeing it plenty. Let's *chust* get this done so we can eat a little something before the horses arrive."

"Eat?" Paul perked up. "Let's hurry, Silas."

In less than twenty minutes, they had the trailer emptied and their driver headed down the road. "We can set up the shop later. The bishop said the stalls were all cleaned out and ready for the horses. They would have helped out more, but the harvest has started in these parts and folks are putting their corn up."

Silas frowned, thinking of the annual harvest party the Beachys hosted. Would they still have it this year? A part of him would miss it, for sure. But another part of him knew how much he'd be aching for Josiah if he were present for it.

He and Josiah had so many years of memories together, and many of their memories centered around harvest time. Like the year they pretended to be scarecrows and frightened the *youngie* exploring the corn maze. Or the time he and Josiah had been in charge of the hayride and the trailer lost a wheel and they had to carry the bishop's *fraa* back. And then there'd been the singing around the campfire and the one time debris flew upward and caught Menno Yoder's hat on fire.

*Ach, Josiah. I miss you so much!*

He couldn't wrap his mind around why *Der Herr* would snatch his best friend in the prime of his life. It *chust* didn't seem fair. He'd tried not to be angry with *Gott*, but it didn't seem to work. He thought about talking to *Dat*, but he would *chust* say he needed to accept it as *Gott's* will and move on.

But Silas wanted real answers. He wanted something he could grasp on to. Something that made sense.

"Silas, we're going to need supplies to fix up the summer kitchen, and I'd like to start on that for your *mamm* as soon as I can. It's still hot yet and we don't need to be heating up that house. If I send you to town with a list, do you think you can handle it?"

"I think so. Do we have a driver yet?"

"I stopped at the phone shanty and there was a number in there. It said Driver Dan. Has truck." *Dat* shrugged. "Sounded like what we need, so I gave him a call. He said he'd be out in about twenty minutes or so. If you can handle that, Paul and I can put the horses up when they arrive."

"Okay. Sounds *gut*." Silas had been curious to see the nearby towns, anyhow. He took the bank card from *Dat*. "Does this work here?"

"I don't see why it shouldn't."

It felt *gut* to have something to do. The more he did, the less time he had to think about how much he missed his best friend.

That was the *gut* thing about being the oldest *kind*. You were trusted with more responsibilities and got to do more stuff than the younger siblings. But *Mamm* and *Dat* had a way of giving each child a task they could manage so each one felt like an important part of the family. Because, as *Mamm* would say, "When young folks have nothing to do, they end up getting into mischief."

# SIXTEEN

As soon as the full-sized midnight-blue pickup truck came to a stop at the end of the driveway, Silas hopped in.

A semi-portly man with graying hair and kind eyes smiled in greeting. "You must be Silas. I'm Driver Dan or Preacher Dan, whichever you'd like to call me is fine. Just don't call me late for supper."

Intrigue piqued Silas's curiosity. He'd never met an *Englisch* preacher. "Preacher Dan? Are you a minister?"

"Retired. I pastored a local church in the community for four decades." He waited for a car to pass by, then pulled out onto the road.

"How does one become an *Englisch* preacher?"

Preacher Dan chuckled. "That all depends on which church you're applying for, I reckon. Some require fancy degrees. I don't have one of those, nor did I ever desire to have one."

"Were you chosen in the lot?"

"Like the Amish do it? No. I guess you could say I was chosen by God."

"How did that happen?"

"God put a Bible in my hand, then laid a burden on my heart for lost souls. And that was that."

"But you preached in a church?"

"Sure did. You see, I was out preaching on the street one day." His grin widened. "Because when the Holy Spirit fills you with His love, you've just gotta share that with somebody. Woo hoo! I knew I was going to Heaven, and I wanted to tell everybody about it so they could go too."

Silas frowned. How did this man *know* he was going to Heaven? Especially since he wasn't even Amish. He never did understand that part.

"Anyhow, I was out there one day, and a man stopped and listened to me preach. I guess he must have liked what I had to say, because he invited me to come preach at his church. They didn't have a pastor at the time, you see. After I'd been there a month or so, they asked me to stay on and become their regular preacher. Stayed for forty-two years."

"And you *wanted* to be a preacher?"

"I know that a lot of the Amish consider being chosen for the ministry to be a burden. But I wanted

God's will for me, and I knew that was what it was."

There it was again. *Gott's* will. "How do you know what *Gott's* will is, though?"

"See that book there?" He pointed to a black leather-bound book on the dash.

Silas guessed it was a Bible. "*Jah.*"

"It holds every answer you'll ever need in this life."

"Every answer?"

Preacher Dan nodded with confidence. "Do you have questions that you need answers to?"

"Lots."

"Do you mind if I ask you a question?"

Silas shook his head.

"If you were to die today, are you one hundred percent sure that you would go to Heaven?"

*Ach*, he'd never had anyone ask him such a direct spiritual question like that. He mulled it over for a moment. He hadn't joined the Amish church yet. And he'd been drinking beer before moving to Indiana. His thoughts toward *Gott* hadn't been all that charitable since Josiah died.

"I don't think so." Silas answered honestly.

"What do you think it takes to get to Heaven?"

"For me or other people?"

"Do you think it's different for you than it is for other people?"

"*Jah*, because I'm Amish."

"Did you know that there are no Amish people in Heaven?"

"What?" He probably said the word a little too loud. How dare this man say such a thing.

"That's right. There are no Amish people in Heaven. Just like there are no Baptist people there. There are no Catholic people there. There are no Protestants."

"Then who *is* there?"

"Grab that book off the dash and open it to the very last book. The Revelation of John."

Silas did as instructed.

"Read chapter twenty-one."

"The whole thing?"

"The whole thing, but pay special attention to the first part of verse twenty-four and verse twenty-seven."

"And the nations of them which are saved shall walk in the light of it." Silas glanced up. "It's talking about Heaven, right?"

"That's right."

He read to the end. "And they which are written in the Lamb's book of life?" Silas looked at Preacher Dan. "How do you know if your name is written in the Lamb's book of life?"

"That is a very good question. Do you know the Lord's Prayer?"

"I know it in German. I'm not sure if I could recite it in English, though."

"It begins with Our Father, which art in Heaven, etcetera."

"*Jah.*"

"So, by the Lord's Prayer, we know that God is in Heaven. And Jesus said, I am the way, the truth, and the life. No man cometh unto the Father but by me." Preacher Dan studied him. "So, life and the way to the Father in Heaven is through Jesus Christ."

"I see."

"Did you, though?"

Silas tilted his head. "What do you mean?"

"Well, that didn't mention any Amish church or Baptist church or Catholic church. There is only one way to Heaven. One way to get your name written in the Lamb's book of life."

"Through Jesus Christ." Silas finished his words.

"Bingo. Christ is all you or I need. That's it."

"That's it? What about being baptized?"

"What about it?"

"I thought a person had to be baptized."

"Do you think the thief on the cross next to Jesus came down off the cross and got baptized?"

"*Nee.* I guess not."

"Silas, I'm going to write down some verses for you. You can look them up on your own or with your family or whoever. If you don't understand them or have questions about them, don't hesitate to call me. God gave us His Word to read and study and understand so we can live in accordance with His will."

"Okay. But why do we get baptized? What is the purpose of it?"

"Baptism is the outward symbol of an inward decision. When you are baptized, which is usually a public thing, you are identifying with Christ. You are saying to the world that you have become a follower of Christ, you have been saved through His blood, and you are now born again, meaning that the old man, your old nature, is dead and buried, and you are now a new creature in Christ."

"I didn't realize it meant all that."

"To put it in Amish terms, it's like a man growing his beard to show that he is married. The beard doesn't make him married, but it is his declaration that it is true. Of course, there are exceptions to this. Like the Swiss Amish who grow a beard as soon as they're able."

"They do? I don't think I've met any Swiss Amish."

"You will see them in these parts. There are a couple of communities not far from here. They also only drive open buggies. For now."

"Even in winter?"

"Even in winter when it's snowing." Preacher Dan merged onto a main highway. "Now, the requirement for baptism is believing in Jesus. You can find that in the book of Acts, chapter eight, verse thirty-seven, where Philip talks with the Ethiopian eunuch. The man asks Philip what hinders him from being baptized. Philip tells the Ethiopian man, *If thou believest with all thine heart, thou mayest.* Then the man said to him, *I believe that Jesus Christ is the Son of God.*

"This verse is important, in my opinion, because it lays out the requirement for baptism. It also lays out what baptism is when it says they went down *into* the water. Just like Jesus did with John the Baptist. When the Bible talks about proper baptism, it always refers to *much* water."

"Does it really matter?"

"It doesn't for salvation. But if you're going to do it, you might as well do it the way the Bible says to."

The presence of stores told Silas they were nearing town. "Are we here?"

"This is Madison. First time here?"

"*Jah.*"

"It's not a big city, but Madison has just about anything you need." He pulled into the home improvement store's parking lot. "Shall we shop, Silas?"

"Let's go."

# SEVENTEEN

S ilas poured over the Bible verses Preacher Dan had given him. *Ach*, they were amazing. How had he not known these things before?

He already considered the older man a friend and confidant. It was strange speaking with him, though. When Silas had a question in the past about things in the church and he'd gone to one of the leaders in his district, he'd never received satisfactory answers.

The answers had been vague or blanket statements, like "We do things this way because that's the way we've always done them." But Silas wanted to know *why* they always did things that way. Was it because of something that was in the Bible, or did someone just make the rule up?

If Preacher Dan had answers to the things they'd already talked about, then maybe he could help Silas find answers to other things that had been on his heart. Things that he'd been struggling with, like Josiah's death.

Someday, he hoped to get answers to all his questions. But right now, he needed to get ready for his first church meeting in their new district.

Sadie Ann Beiler couldn't help but notice that the new family had an eligible *sohn* that would likely be attending the young folks' gathering tonight. There had been rumors floating around the community about the family from Pennsylvania, so she knew a little bit about them.

She couldn't be sure if the rumors were true or not, but it had been mentioned that the family had moved after a death. Had one of the family members passed away? If so, her heart went out to them. She'd lost her younger *bruder* in a farm accident just a few years ago. It had been a hard pill to swallow, but life continued to march on as though it never even happened. It was strange how that worked.

As the Stoltzfus's house was transformed from church meeting to dining area, nervousness pricked Sadie Ann. A part of her hoped she wouldn't have to deliver food to the table where the men from the new family sat. Another part hoped she would get a chance to catch the oldest Miller boy's eye before any other girl did.

She didn't know why, though. It wasn't as though a handsome young man like that would give her the time of day. Not if he knew about her past mistakes.

*Nee*, she'd be better off steering clear of him. Let one of the other *maed* in their district catch his eye.

Silas hadn't really been looking for a *maedel*, but there had been one pretty girl in particular he couldn't help but notice. Had *Der Herr* put her in his line of vision on purpose?

He'd first noticed her during the service, but now that they'd both finally sat down to eat, he had a perfect view of her. She'd glanced up once or twice and he thought their eyes had connected. Then she quickly looked away.

One of the young men near his age bumped his shoulder. "I see you've noticed Sadie Ann Beiler."

"Is that the name of the woman sitting near the end?"

"Yep, that's her. But you shouldn't get any romantic notions about her. She's not really the type of *maedel* a body wants to marry."

Silas frowned at the young man. That had been a

rude thing to say. "Why not?"

"Just trust me. She isn't."

When Silas glanced up again, Sadie Ann had scurried away.

He sighed. He guessed that if he wanted to get to know her better, then he'd have to show up at the singing tonight—something he had no desire to do.

"Are you going with the *youngie* tonight?" *Mamm* called over her shoulder as their family traveled home from meeting.

Silas thought of the gatherings in his former district and how much fun he and Josiah had. The thought of attending alone pained his heart. He wondered if everything would always remind him of his best friend. "*Nee.*"

*Mamm* turned in her seat now. "Whyever not, *sohn*?"

"Let him be, Dory." *Dat* spoke up for him. "He can make his own choices."

Silas was thankful for *Dat's* words.

"I saw him looking at a pretty *maedel*." Paul volunteered. "She was looking at him, too."

Leave it to Paul to tell. Silas nudged his *bruder* in disapproval.

"I think you should go, *sohn*." *Mamm* urged.

"He already said *nee*, Dory. Leave it at that," *Dat* said, then glanced back at his *bruder*. "And Paul, you mind your own beeswax."

# EIGHTEEN

To Silas's delight, Preacher Dan had become one of his family's regular drivers. And since Silas was the main gopher at the construction site he and *Dat* now worked at, he had ample opportunities to converse with Preacher Dan.

"Tell me your story, Silas." Preacher Dan encouraged.

"What do you want to know?"

"Let's just start with why you wear a permanent frown. I don't think I've seen you smile once since we've met. Not even when I cracked a joke." Now it was Preacher Dan's turn to frown.

The truth was, Silas didn't feel like he had all that much to smile about anymore. He never realized how much happiness Josiah brought to his life. Now, all he felt was a void in that part of his soul. And he was unsure it could ever be filled.

"I lost my best friend a month and a half ago. He drowned in the ocean." It was still so painful to utter those words. One would think the pain would lessen with time, but it hadn't. Not yet.

"Ah, that explains it. I'm so sorry for your loss, Silas. Losing someone close to you is hard."

"You know, it's strange. The ocean seemed so peaceful before Josiah drowned. Afterward, there was no peace to be found."

"Do you know why you didn't feel calm at the ocean? Peace doesn't come from a place. It comes from a person."

Silas frowned. "A person?"

The preacher nodded. "Jesus Christ. He said, *Peace I leave with you, my peace I give unto you: not as the world giveth, give I unto you. Let not your heart be troubled, neither let it be afraid.* You see, we can't have true peace apart from Jesus Christ. He is the only one who can give us true, everlasting peace."

Silas recalled the verses they'd read on their previous trip. "And He is the one who gives us eternal life and writes our name in the book of life."

"I certainly don't claim to know everything about the Bible, but I believe every person's name is written in the book of life from the time they are created. And when they reject Christ's sacrifice for their sins, their name is then blotted out."

"I hadn't considered that."

"The Bible says that God is not willing that *any* should perish but that *all* should come to repentance. His will is Heaven for everybody. That's why Christ died. However, God gives human beings a choice in the matter. He does not force us to do something we don't want to, even if it's for our own good."

"Why do people go to hell? I never understood that part about God and His plan."

"I like your questions, Silas. I can tell you're a thinker." Preacher Dan smiled. "According to the Bible, hell exists for the punishment of evildoers. It was prepared for the devil and his angels. People were never meant to go there. That's why God made salvation so simple for us."

Silas pondered his words. "Growing up Amish, I always thought I had to be Amish or stay Amish to have any hope of Heaven. But from what I'm reading, Heaven doesn't seem to have anything to do with Amish or not."

"That's right. What people need to realize is that their relationship with God is between them and God, and no one else. You are supposed to work out *your own* salvation with fear and trembling. When you stand before God at the end of this life, it will be you and God. Not you and your church and God. Not you and your spouse or friends and God. Not you and your folks and God. You. God. Period."

Preacher Dan continued. "Everything you say and do is ultimately between you and Him. Nobody else may see your sins or know about them. But God sees and knows *everything*. There is nothing hidden from Him."

Preacher Dan glanced at him. "So, when Jesus washes our sins away, that is a big deal. Because that future day when you have to stand before your Maker just got a whole lot easier. When you stand before Him then, it won't just be you and God. Christ will be standing right there with you. The Bible says that He is our Advocate and our Mediator."

Silas scratched his head. "I'm not quite sure I know what those words mean."

"An advocate is basically a friend who will stick up for you. And a mediator is one who stands between two parties and negotiates. So, it's like you, Jesus, and God standing in Heaven—or I don't know, maybe God will be sitting on His throne—and Jesus throws His arm around your shoulders and speaks up for you and says, "He's cool, Dad. He's with Me.'"

Silas smiled now. "I like that thought." Then he frowned. "But what happens when someone never accepts Jesus?"

"That's where the book of life comes in. If they've rejected His free gift, His payment for their sins, then they will have to pay for their own sins. And I'm afraid that price is too high for anyone, but Christ, to pay. Because their name was blotted out, those people will stand before God with Jesus Christ as their judge instead of their advocate."

"That sounds frightening."

"It is. The Bible says it is a fearful thing to fall into the hands of the living God. Without Christ, the only recourse is hell. That's why God's Word also says that *now* is the day of salvation. It isn't something that should be put off till later. None of us knows if our next breath will be our last or whether we'll live on this earth fifty more years. But there are people who die suddenly all the time. We are admonished not to harden our hearts because the opportunity can vanish just like that." He snapped his fingers.

Just like Josiah. His time was up, and he had no more opportunities to make his life right with *Der Herr*. The thought saddened Silas. He hoped and prayed that Josiah's fate would not be hell.

"Preacher Dan, I want to be saved, but I don't think I understand it all."

He chuckled. "Silas, none of us understand it all. That's God's business. But He allows us to understand what we need to know."

A sigh escaped Silas's lips. This was all so much to take in. "The hard part for me, I guess, is that I've been taught that saying that you know you are saved is prideful. And pride is what made the devil fall. Only God can know."

"Silas." Preacher Dan shook his head. "You've been taught wrong. The Bible must always be where our answers come from. They cannot come from man.

"The only way salvation can be prideful is if you've earned it yourself, and the Bible tells us salvation cannot be earned. That is the whole point of the Gospel. Jesus paid for our sins because it was something we *couldn't* do on our own. The Apostle Paul said he boasts in the Lord. He was a religious person too, willing to do anything for what he believed was right. Then God had to show him that what he thought was right was actually wrong. Believing something with all your heart doesn't make it right."

Silas blew out a breath. "How can we know the truth, then?"

"That's why God gave us His Word. It is the source of all truth. And isn't it interesting that *Jesus said, I am the way, the truth, and the life*? And isn't it interesting that Jesus is referred to as the Word of God? *In the beginning was the Word, and the Word was with God, and the Word was God.* If we are searching for truth, we need to look no further than God's Word. Everything must be tested by the Bible. If it doesn't line up, we must throw it out."

"So, it isn't prideful to say that you know you are saved?"

"*These things have I written unto you that believe on the name of the Son of God; that ye may know that ye have eternal life.* That verse comes from First John. Now, do you suppose God would have included it in the Bible if He didn't want us to know? It seems to me that he gave John those words because He wanted us to have assurance of eternal life."

"*Ach*, I've never read that verse. But it makes perfect sense."

"The one thing the devil is good at is getting folks to doubt God's Word. That's how the fall of man began in the Garden of Eden. Satan made Eve question what God said."

"It's so easy to be led down the wrong path, ain't so?"

"Unfortunately, yes, if we don't know what God's Word says. That's why it's so important to study."

"I want to know that I'm saved, Preacher Dan."

"Well, that part is easy." The preacher smiled. "*For whosoever shall call upon the name of the Lord shall be saved.*"

# NINETEEN

It was the strangest thing. Silas felt like a brand-new person.

*Nee*, all of his troubles hadn't vanished away, but now he possessed hope beyond anything he could ever imagine. The world around him looked brighter. It was as though he'd been given new eyes.

The days ahead no longer seemed dark and hopeless. God had a plan for him, and Silas was confident that God would fulfill His purpose in him.

"You're smiling now." Paul remarked on their way to school.

*Mamm* had insisted Silas drive the *kinner* to school because she didn't trust Paul's driving on the rollercoaster road, as their family had aptly nicknamed it.

"*Jah*, I guess I am. *Der Herr* has given me peace in my heart."

"Well, I'm glad, because I didn't like seeing you sad all the time. It was almost like *mei bruder* had died with his best friend. I'm glad to have you back."

Paul's words pierced Silas's heart, because they were true. He'd nearly let grief swallow him up and suck all the life out of him. "I'm glad to be back. But I still miss Josiah something wonderful."

"I don't think that is something that goes away, ain't not?"

Silas sighed. "I imagine not. And that's probably the way it should be. No one should ever be forgotten." He pulled the rig into the school yard.

"Well, look who's here." Paul nudged Silas. "It's the *maedel* from meeting who caught your eye."

Silas's gaze went to the young woman, who seemed to be dropping off her younger siblings, as he was. He smiled, and when she'd reciprocated, he lifted a hand in her direction.

The *kinner* scrambled from the buggy as Silas bid them farewell for the day. When he headed down the road, he noticed Sadie Ann had ventured off in the opposite direction.

He smiled to himself. Maybe he would have an opportunity to get to know her at the next young folks' gathering.

When Silas returned home, he discovered *Dat* had gone to the construction site without him today. Apparently, *Mamm* had tasks for Silas at home, which was fine with him.

"I have a list of things I need you to fetch from the store," *Mamm* informed him. "I've already called the driver. He'll be here soon to pick you up."

"Okay." Shopping wasn't exactly his favorite task, but there were worse things *Mamm* could have asked him to do. Like watch the *boppli* while she went to the store. Last time that happened, little Emily had cried nearly the entire time. Silas hadn't known what to do and he'd felt helpless. It wasn't until *Mamm* returned that the *boppli* calmed down. The entire ordeal had felt like a nightmare that he didn't wish to repeat.

"Driver's here!" *Mamm* called. "You've got the list, ain't so?"

"*Jah.*"

"Okay, follow it closely. Be sure to get exactly what's written down."

"I'll do my best, *Mamm*." Silas stepped out the door but was surprised to see a different vehicle than Preacher Dan's truck. He opened the door to the vehicle to discover another driver. He swallowed down his disappointment. "I thought Dan was coming today."

Jennifer Spredemann

He spoke the words figuring the drivers knew each other. That was the way it had been in his former district. Most of the Amish taxi drivers, unless they were new to driving the Amish, knew each other.

"I'm Joe, Preacher Dan's son. And this is my wife, Tattie."

"I see." Was this man anything like his father? "*Gut* to meet you. I'm Silas."

"We've heard all about you." Tattie smiled. "My father-in-law is quite fond of you."

The sentiments were the same. He had great respect for Preacher Dan.

But his son's name was Joe? Just like the shortened version he and his friends had used for Josiah. His heart clenched once again, but the despair he'd felt before was no longer there. He would miss his friend for as long as he lived, but *Der Herr* had allowed him to come to peace with Josiah's tragedy.

"My wife and I were already on our way into town, so Dad asked me to swing by and pick you up." Joe glanced back at him. "I hope you don't mind, but we have another person to pick up too."

Did Joe just wink at his wife? "We figured since you're both going to Madison alone, we may as well make the most out of it."

Silas nodded. Personally, he'd rather go alone but

154

who was he to tell his *Englisch* driver what to do?

A few moments later, they pulled into a driveway.

To his dismay, Sadie Ann emerged from the Amish farmhouse. All of a sudden, the car felt warm.

As she entered the vehicle, her eyes widened. Apparently, she hadn't been expecting him either. "Hi," she said as she slid into the backseat next to him then buckled her seatbelt.

"Do you two know each other?" Tattie turned from the front seat to smile at them.

"No, we've never met," Silas said, glancing at Sadie Ann. "I'm Silas Miller."

"Sadie Ann Beiler." *Ach*, her smile was lovely. "Are you going to Walmart too?"

"*Jah, Mamm* sent me with a list." He showed it to Sadie Ann.

She laughed, then their conversation automatically switched to their native language. "That looks a lot like mine."

"Maybe you can help me, then, because I've never been to this Walmart and I have no idea where to find all this stuff." He admitted.

"I'd be happy to."

"*Denki*, I appreciate it."

Tattie entered their conversation. "Joe and I like to stop in at the buffet while we're in town. Would you two like to go along?"

Sadie Ann's eyes lit up. "The Chinese buffet?"

"Yes." Tattie confirmed.

"I'd love to go, if Silas wants to." She grinned, then turned to him. "Their food is delicious. Most of the folks in our community love to go there."

Silas shrugged. "Sounds *gut* to me. I can always eat."

By the time their shopping excursion was over, Silas felt like he and Sadie Ann had established a friendship of sorts. They'd shopped together, eaten together, and even laughed together.

When Joe and Tattie dropped Sadie Ann off, Silas knew he needed to seize the opportunity to ask her about the next young folks' gathering.

"I don't really know anyone in this community yet, so I was hoping you could maybe introduce me to some of the young folks." He ventured.

"Sure, I can do that." She nodded.

"And also, would you let me take you home from the singing on Sunday?" *Ach*, but what if she already had a beau? "I mean, if you don't have a ride yet."

Her smile was genuine. "I'd like that, Silas."

As she slid out of the vehicle, his heart felt like it

was beating a hundred miles per hour. Her siblings rushed out to help carry the groceries inside, then they were headed off back home. Silas had been thankful that Joe and Tattie had taken both of them.

Had they orchestrated the meeting or had *Der Herr*?

# TWENTY

Sadie Ann had gone through her dresses several times now. If only she knew what Silas's favorite color was. If she did, it would be a lot easier to choose a dress for the singing tonight.

She nibbled on her lip. The other *maed* wouldn't be pleased when they discovered the newest eligible bachelor had chosen *her* to ride with him tonight.

She frowned. Maybe she should have declined his offer and let him ask another *maedel*. She wasn't worthy of his attention.

A part of her was surprised that word about her hadn't gotten around to him yet. She'd seen him sitting next to Jacob Yoder. It would be a miracle if Jacob hadn't said anything. Jacob had been friends with Michael Eicher, who had surely bragged about their dates. *Ach*, she'd been such a fool to fall for Michael Eicher's *gut* looks.

Now, she wished she'd never even met the handsome *bu* who skipped town and dropped her like a hot potato.

A part of her didn't want Silas to ever find out about Michael, but another part knew that if he pursued a relationship with her, he had a right to know.

She didn't know why she was worried about it. Chances were, he'd dump her the moment he found out anyhow. Either that, or he'd do his best to take advantage of her like other boys had tried to.

That was why, up until now, she hadn't accepted any more invitations to ride with any of the *buwe* in the *g'may*. But there had been something different about Silas Miller, and she hoped that just maybe he was different than the other *buwe* in the community who'd expressed an interest in her.

Perhaps it was unfair to judge this new Amish community by his former one. Maybe it was different because he'd grown up around the people in Pennsylvania, so he felt comfortable with them. Or were these people standoffish with him because he'd come with Sadie Ann? He couldn't be sure.

When he'd joined the volleyball game, he hadn't

been prepared for the memories of Josiah and their *rumspringa* trip to come rushing back. He had a hard time focusing on the game. Perhaps he hadn't been ready to join the *youngie* just yet.

He'd been glad when Sadie Ann suggested they leave as soon as was proper. She hadn't seemed all that comfortable around the young folks either, and he wondered why. Hadn't she grown up here?

He held the reins tight as she hopped up onto the seat. "*Denki* for introducing me to your friends."

"You're welcome."

He scratched his cheek. "I don't really know how to say this, so I'm *chust* going to come out with it."

"Should I be worried?"

"Maybe." He shrugged. "I'm not the type of person to beat around the bush, so here's the thing. I don't have in mind to attend singings for years and years and date every *maedel* in the *g'may*. I want to get hitched without a lot of drama."

Her eyes widened.

"I know this sounds forward, but if you don't think it's something you're interested in, then this will be our first and last date." He sighed. "You may have heard that my best friend in Pennsylvania died a couple of months ago."

She gasped. "*Ach*, I had heard someone close had

161

died, but I didn't know who." She touched his hand. "Silas, I'm so sorry."

"I'm not going to lie. His death was very hard on me. But it made me realize how fleeting life is. And that's why I don't want to go through all the drama with finding someone. I think that finding the right mate isn't as important as being the right mate. Any couple can make a relationship work if they choose to, if they are willing. Do you know what I mean?"

"*Jah*, I think so. I actually like your way of thinking."

"You do?" He chuckled. "I thought I may have scared you off already."

"There's nothing wrong with knowing what you want."

"The fact is I'm attracted to you and, what I know of you, I like."

"I feel the same way about you. But Silas, I've made some mistakes in my past."

He shrugged. "We all have. I'm not concerned about your past. If you want to tell me about it, you can, but don't feel like you have to. I have done things in my past that I am ashamed of. But they are in my past and I've moved on."

"I've moved on too, but I feel like other people judge me because of it."

"Ignore other people. The only person you need to be pleasing to is *Der Herr*. His opinion of us is all that matters."

"You know what? You're right."

"Feel free to ask me anything. My life is an open book."

"How old are you?"

"I'm nineteen. How about you?"

"Seventeen. Is that too young for you?"

He smiled. "*Nee*, I don't think so. I'd say you're about perfect for me." His eyes scanned her briefly.

Her cheeks turned a lovely shade of pink and he had the overwhelming urge to kiss her. *Ach*, where had that come from?

"What is your favorite color?" she asked.

"I like many colors, but that dress brings out your pretty blue eyes."

"Silas Miller, are you trying to flatter me?"

"I only speak the truth. And maybe a little." He teased. "I hope to get a kiss by the end of the night."

That remark caused her to laugh out loud. "I guess you really do speak your mind."

"Since we're on the subject of kissing, I also want to be upfront about something else."

"What's that?" She swallowed.

"Until we are hitched, I have no plans for sharing the marriage bed."

Sadie Ann frowned. "Did you think that I *do* have plans?"

*Ach*, he hoped he hadn't offended her. "Not at all. I *chust* want you to feel comfortable with me and know that I won't expect that from you. Trust me, I have a lot of friends back in Pennsylvania, both Amish and *Englisch*, and I know how they can be. I'm not one of those guys."

"I think I'm in love with you already."

He knew she only meant it as a joke, but he was happy to put her mind at ease. "Do you think you could love me for real someday?" He said in all seriousness.

"Silas Miller, I'm sure of it."

"*Gut*. Because I know I can love you too."

# TWENTY-ONE

Kayla felt fatter every day. If she ever got her
hands on Josiah Beachy again, she would wring
his neck. Or kiss him. She wasn't quite sure.
Because, while she was put out with him for
abandoning her, she still couldn't help but love him—
or who she thought he was.

If only he would show up on her doorstep! She
would forgive everything with just a word from him.
Anything. She just wanted to know that she wasn't
alone in this. She didn't want to raise *their* baby alone.
Didn't a child need both a mother and a father?

She still held out hope for Josiah. A hundred things
could have happened. Like Sierra suggested, he could
have lost her contact information.

If only she had a way to let him know that she was
expecting his baby.

She shoved away the tears. God knew she must've

shed thousands over him by now. Speaking of God, where was He? Why wouldn't He answer her prayers for help in finding Josiah?

This was all so unfair. Not just to her, but to Josiah too. What if he'd want to know that he had a baby on the way?

She'd dropped out of school when she started showing, opting for home study instead of dealing with high school gossip. Sierra had helped her make that decision. She didn't need that kind of negativity in her life, especially with a little one on the way.

She'd had an ultrasound several weeks ago and discovered she was expecting a little girl. As her belly grew large, she wondered what this little one would look like. Would she look anything like her daddy? How would Josiah respond to a little girl in his likeness?

Kayla sighed. She might as well come to terms with reality. Josiah Beachy, if that was even his real name, was never coming back. It was time to grieve the death of their relationship once and for all and put it behind her. Time to stop the fantasies about him finding her and the three of them becoming a family. It wasn't going to happen.

She thought about the photos she still had. Although she'd considered tossing them out, she wouldn't. One day, her daughter might have questions. She deserved at least some answers. She would tuck them away for the future. It was quite possible that she'd never pull them out again, but who could guess what might lie up ahead?

She had a future to look forward to. One where an innocent little girl would be counting on her. She needed to be strong. She needed to set the past aside and pour every ounce of love she had into the life of her little girl.

And that was exactly what she determined to do. If Kayla had anything to say about it, Bailey Jo Johnson would be the most loved little girl that ever lived. Bailey, because Kayla just liked the name, and Jo after her father. She'd keep the name Johnson just in case Beachy wasn't her father's real last name. Kayla still had her suspicions.

Was it possible that Bailey would someday meet her father? It was anybody's guess.

# TWENTY-TWO

As the buggy traveled down the road, Silas thought of his and Sadie Ann's relationship. He'd been right. They made a *gut* match.

"Is the heater warm enough for you?" He glanced at his *aldi*, wrapped in her wool shawl, and covered with his lap robe. It had been a cold night—the perfect setting for the upcoming Christmas festivities.

"*Jah*, I'm *gut*. It will be fun watching the *kinner* perform their parts in the Christmas program." She shivered and he draped his arm around her.

"I don't know how Paul will do with a serious part. I hope he doesn't butcher it."

"If he does, it will make it all the more memorable, ain't so?"

Silas chuckled. "I guess you're right. *Chust* don't tell Paul that or he'll mess it up on purpose."

"I think *mei schweschder* might have a crush on him.

She's excited that she gets to play the part of Mary alongside him. I don't doubt that she's imagined they really are Mary and Joseph and are married."

Silas reached for Sadie Ann's gloved hand and encased it in his own. "That's cute. But I'm sorry to say, he probably hasn't even noticed her. As far as I know, Paul has zero interest in *maed* right now."

"Do you think he'll give her a hard time if she gives him a gift? I think she made him cookies."

"Well, I know he won't refuse the cookies. Hopefully, he doesn't say anything *dumm* to hurt her feelings." He glanced around to be sure they were the only ones on the road, then leaned over and grazed her cheek with a kiss. "*Ach*, your cheeks are cold."

"All of me is cold." She laughed. "You'll have to warm me up later."

He raised a brow and grinned. "With pleasure."

"*Ach*, look! It's snowing!"

"It is. We might have a slick ride home tonight."

"We can take our time."

"I was going to ask. Would you like to come over on Second Christmas and take supper with my family?" Silas hoped Sadie Ann would say yes.

She smiled in return. "I'd love to."

"I *chust* have to warn you about my *bruder*, Paul. He likes to tease me."

She waved a hand in front of her face. "I'm used to that. You should meet my *dat*."

"I have talked to him a couple of times at meeting. It looks like you'll fit right in with *mei familye* then. *Gut*."

Kayla had been dreading spending Christmas with her aunts and uncles in Washington, so she'd used her pregnancy as an excuse to stay home while Mom and Dad traveled across state lines. To tell the truth, she didn't want to face everyone like this.

She had no desire for people to stare at her in judgment. Heaven knew, she'd done that enough to herself plenty over the past few months. She didn't need anyone else to.

Living in a different state, she'd never been close to them anyhow. The only thing she'd miss, besides her parents, was the snow. Where they lived in California, they'd never had snow at Christmas. Or any other time of the year, for that matter.

She wondered about Josiah. Was he sitting around a beautifully decorated Christmas tree with his big, happy family in his farmhouse? She could picture it now. The Christmas lights flickering. The snow falling outside the windows of his Pennsylvania home. Because surely they had snow for Christmas in Pennsylvania, didn't they?

That was something she'd love to be a part of—being surrounded by a big, happy family. Having her own husband and children. She'd likely never have that. Because what kind of decent man would want to marry her with all her issues?

A tear slipped down her cheek. While Josiah was probably having the time of his life, she was here spending Christmas all alone.

Just then, the life inside her pushed against her belly, reminding her that she wasn't alone. This little girl would never know a Christmas deprived of love. Kayla would make sure of that.

As a matter of fact, this little one deserved some Christmas cookies. She smiled to herself. Yes, she and Bailey would celebrate the season with just the two of them, and that would be enough.

Just then, the phone rang. The first couple of months after she'd returned home from New Jersey, she would have rushed to answer it, hoping it would be Josiah. Now, she had no such notions.

"Kayla?"

She smiled as Sierra's voice sang over the phone. "Hi, Sierra."

"What are you doing?"

"Bailey and I were just about to bake some cookies." She rubbed her midsection and smiled.

"Well, hold off on dessert because I just stopped by In-N-Out and I've got animal fries to deliver."

Happiness tipped Kayla's lips. "Have I told you that you're the best friend ever?"

"Only a thousand times, but you can say it again."

"Well, I'm glad you're coming because I have a gift for you. I hoped I'd see you before your family went out of town. When are you leaving to see your grandma?"

"In about thirty minutes."

Kayla's eyes bulged. "Oh, you don't have much time."

"I know."

Several minutes later, the doorbell rang, and Kayla rushed to let Sierra in. Fortunately, she had her friend's gift all wrapped up and ready to go. Unfortunately, Sierra wouldn't have time to open it.

Sierra handed Kayla the special fries she'd been craving all throughout her pregnancy. "Eat them now while they're still fresh." She handed her a small box. "This is for you and the baby. Open it later."

"Here's your gift. Let me know how you like it." She'd wrapped the garment box in purple, Sierra's favorite color.

Sierra enveloped Kayla in a hug. "I'll call you later! Enjoy your fries. Merry Christmas! Love you."

Kayla couldn't suppress her smile. Because even though she was expecting a baby out-of-wedlock, even though she didn't know where Bailey's father was, even though she'd be spending Christmas alone, she still had a bright future and lot to be thankful for.

And that was what she would focus on this season.

# EPILOGUE

Silas sucked in a deep breath. Today was bittersweet. It was the day he and Sadie Ann would be baptized into the Amish church. He'd always pictured this day with his best friend at his side. But his best friend wasn't here. He wondered if *chust* maybe Josiah was watching from Heaven.

Was that even a thing? He'd have to ask Preacher Dan about that.

Silas had lost a *gut* friend in Josiah, but he'd gained a couple of new ones in the fallout.

His eyes connected with Sadie Anne—the woman whom he'd fallen in love with. He couldn't wait to take her as his bride this year. He could only wonder what *Der Herr* had planned for their future. But maybe it was best not knowing. Maybe it was best to trust *Der Herr* with *chust* one day at a time.

Comfort filled his heart as he thought of the words

Preacher Dan had shared with him. "We may not always understand the why, but we can trust the Who."

With everything in him, with everything that would come to pass in his life, Silas determined that he would trust the Who.

## THE END

If you haven't read the AMISH COUNTRY
BRIDES Series, you'll want to continue reading with

# The Trespasser

*Amish Country Brides*

Jennifer Spredemann

© 2019

# CHAPTER ONE

Kayla Johnson squinted to see through the windshield as her wipers attempted to keep up with the torrential downpour assaulting her vehicle. But even with the wipers at full speed, that proved to be a challenge. She wasn't even sure where she and Bailey were exactly, but they'd crossed the state line from Kentucky into Indiana about an hour ago, or so it seemed. She distinctly remembered the 'Welcome to Indiana' sign just as they'd crossed the bridge over the gigantic Ohio River.

Perhaps she should pull over somewhere and wait out the storm. She couldn't tell if she was even going the right way, since her GPS had lost its signal several miles back. She figured it was due to the storm raging outside. How long would this last? *Now* she understood when people mentioned the storms in the Midwest. This was downright terrifying.

As if on cue, a streak of lightning touched down just off to the left. Not even five seconds later, thunder shook her car. A shiver raced up her spine.

"I'm scared, Mommy," Bailey whimpered from her booster seat in the backseat.

*Me too.* "It's okay, baby. Mommy's going to pull off up here." She'd hoped to find a motel or a fast food restaurant, but who knew how far she was from one. The last town had several, but she'd spotted them before the sky began dumping buckets of water. She hadn't expected *this*. If she'd known this was coming, she would have reserved a hotel room in the last town, and she and her five-year-old daughter would be safe and sound, curled up under the covers watching a family-friendly movie.

She flipped on her signal and maneuvered onto the next street. Great, no lines to even mark the road? She must be out in the middle of nowhere. The vehicle crawled at a snail's pace as she struggled to see the road ahead of her. It seemed to be at least a couple of inches deep in water. They really needed to get out of this. Was that a little store up ahead? She couldn't be sure since there were no lights on, but they were probably closed. 'Yoder's Country Market' the sign on the small white building read. *Yoder*. Wasn't that an *Amish* name? As she pulled into the drive, she discovered a chain-link fence surrounding the parking lot. Definitely closed.

She sighed.

"I need to go to the bathroom," Bailey whined.

"Okay. I think there might be a house down this driveway. We'll stop and ask to use their restroom." She drove along what appeared to be a fenced pasture. Or was it a small pond? It was difficult to tell with all the water everywhere.

Her cell phone began vibrating. No doubt another storm warning. She briefly glanced at it. *Flash flood warning*. Great. Perhaps the residents would allow her and Bailey to stay a while. She hoped so, because being out in this weather set her nerves on edge.

She pulled up to a large white two-story house. Should she just stop in front, or find a place to park out of the rain? She opted for the latter when she noticed a couple of structures independent of the house. A barn and another outbuilding of some sort. She slowly crept up to the smaller structure, hoping there was an empty spot large enough to house her vehicle.

Thunder rumbled overhead once again.

"Please, Mommy! I gotta go!"

"Okay, baby." As soon as she pulled under the outbuilding's roof, she could see clearly enough to park. She spotted a hitching post. *This must be where they park the buggies.* Except, there were no buggies present. Perhaps they were in the massive barn. Hopefully, the owners wouldn't mind her parking her car there.

Kayla opened the door, then went to release Bailey from her booster seat. "Do you think you can wait for Mommy to find the umbrella? It's just in my suitcase."

"I think so. But please hurry!" Bailey slid out of the car, then bounced up and down.

"I will." She quickly popped the trunk open and rifled through her clothing. She grabbed a comfortable change of clothes for each of them, just in case they were allowed to stay a while. "Okay. You ready to make a run for the door?"

"Yep."

"One. Two. Three." With the clothing tucked under her arm, she held the umbrella in one hand and Bailey's hand in the other, then made a mad dash for the front door.

"Whew!" She glanced down at her jeans near her ankles. They were completely soaked. It was a good thing she'd thought to grab extra outfits for the two of them. It would take a while for her tennis shoes to dry, however.

She knocked on the door loudly so it would be heard over the pounding rain. Didn't it ever let up? It seemed not.

No answer. She knocked again, harder this time.

"Mommy!" Bailey bounced.

"Okay, okay. I don't think anyone's home. I don't feel right just going inside."

"Maybe no one lives here anymore or they're on vacation like us." Bailey turned the knob, and the door opened. She rushed inside before Kayla could stop her.

"Bailey!"

"I have to go potty!"

Kayla gingerly stepped into the house and looked around the dark room. Indeed, it appeared empty. "Hello? Is anybody home?"

No answer.

"My daughter needs to use the restroom," she called out, stepping further inside. "Hello!"

Silence answered back. No one was home.

"Okay, we'll quickly find the bathroom, then we'll leave." She felt for a light switch but found none. *Oh, yeah. Amish. No electricity.*

A flash of lightning illuminated what appeared to be the living area, revealing sparse furniture covered in white sheets. It was as though the occupants had moved. But why would they leave the door unlocked?

"Where will we go?" Bailey's frightened voice commanded her attention once again.

"I don't know, baby. Maybe...let's just find the bathroom so you don't pee your pants." She released a sigh of relief. If nobody was home, if the house was unoccupied, perhaps hunkering down here for an evening might be an option. But still, it wasn't her home. And how would she feel if a stranger occupied her place of residence in her absence? Not that she currently had a place of residence.

She walked through the darkened home. Thankfully, it wasn't pitch black. There should be a lantern somewhere, shouldn't there be? Perhaps not, if the owners no longer occupied the place. She scolded herself for not thinking to grab the flashlight out of the glove compartment. Of course, she hadn't expected to find a dark empty house. She'd run back out to get it if buckets of water weren't dumping from the sky.

She felt her way into the main living area until her eyes adjusted. Another flash of lightning revealed a kitchen off to one side. As she walked further inside the home, a quick perusal indicated a bedroom stood off to the other side, along a short hallway that led to stairs. Perhaps the bathroom adjoined the bedroom.

She peered inside the empty room. No, it didn't appear to.

"I found it!" Bailey hollered.

A door slammed shut. Whew! At least now she didn't have to worry about Bailey having an accident.

Once her eyes adjusted a little more, she spotted a lone lantern on a small table. Oh, good, a book of matches sat next to it. She quickly removed the hurricane glass, turned up the wick, then swiped a match to light it. A soft glow dispelled the darkness.

Fortunately, she'd come from a family of campers, so she was familiar with lighting lanterns, setting up tents, chopping wood, kindling a campfire, and other outdoor skills. Sadness filled her as she thought of Mom and Dad and all the wonderful times they'd spent camping. They'd passed away much too early. Did anyone survive cancer these days? It seemed not.

She briefly toured the lower level of the home with the lantern in hand, noting a few bedrooms. Two of them had lone beds in them, one covered by a quilt and the other with a plain comforter. Would the owners mind if she and Bailey occupied the rooms for a night? Since there seemed to be no one around to ask, she'd have to take a chance. What other choice did they have?

Thunder roared outside once again along with

pounding rain. It appeared they wouldn't be going anywhere anytime soon. Not with all the flash flood warnings and lightning strikes. It just wasn't safe. Or smart.

Had Someone up above provided this shelter from the storm? It was possible, she supposed, but definitely not probable. The Man Upstairs didn't care about her or Bailey, she'd been certain of that since she first discovered her pregnancy. And then she'd lost both parents.

No, it certainly wasn't God. Finding this place had been pure luck, plain and simple.

# CHAPTER TWO

S ilas Miller dashed for the shelter of the barn. He hated to take Strider out in this weather, but he needed to check the Yoders' gutters to make sure they were free of debris. It was times like this he was thankful his Amish community allowed enclosed buggies. The nearby Swiss Amish district, nicknamed the Swissies by local Plain folks, only utilized open-top carriages. He couldn't imagine weathering this menacing storm with a simple umbrella as protection. At least he was protected from the elements.

He quickly harnessed Strider, moved him between the traces, making sure to guide them into their proper places, and then pulled the leather reins into the buggy's cab. Fortunately, his horse loved the rain. Unfortunately, Strider did not love thunder and lightning.

Strider whinnied, excited to be leaving his barn stall, no doubt. He might have a change of mind once they got out onto the road and encountered a loud crash of thunder like the one several minutes ago. Maybe *Der Herr* would have mercy on poor Strider and hold off the lightning until they arrived at the Yoders'. He'd pray for that.

"Come on, boy. We won't be out too long, but it'll be enough to invigorate you." He gave the lines a gentle shake, urging Strider to begin their three-mile journey.

It seemed like the rain had let up a tiny bit, but it still poured. He just hoped the driver of the car up ahead spotted him and slowed down. This road was quite narrow and, in some places, had no room to pull off to the side. He double checked to make sure his blinking lights were on. He pulled to the right as much as possible to allow the car to pass.

He sighed in relief once it did. Hopefully, no one else was crazy enough to be out in this weather. He wouldn't be either, but he'd promised Dan Yoder that he'd look after his place after their family had moved back to Pennsylvania. Dan, the minister of their district, had talked about selling the place on more than one occasion, but for whatever reason, it had yet to go up for sale. And for that, Silas was happy. He'd dreamed about having his own acreage, complete with a large barn, and a small store in the front, since he'd been finished with school. The Yoders' property would be the perfect place, but he was in no position finance-wise to buy it. Nowhere near, actually. But he had been saving his money. And praying that the house wouldn't sell to anyone else.

As he neared the two-mile mark, he noticed something up ahead. *Ach,* the creek had swollen considerably.

"Do you think we can do it, Strider?"

The horse lifted his head as though in agreement.

"Okay, but we'll have to be careful."

He approached the water cautiously and urged Strider along. "Come on, boy. You can do this." He slapped the reins a little firmer. "Let's go!"

The horse waded through the water adequately, but the buggy still weighed him down. Silas encouraged the horse again and glanced out the side flap. The water reached the middle of his buggy's wheel. If it were any higher, Strider wouldn't be able to pull through.

Once they were safely past the creek, he exhaled in relief. It proved to be swifter than he'd surmised. Getting back home would be a chore if the creek rose any higher. As a matter of fact, maybe he'd use the Yoders' phone shanty and leave a message on the line closest to his folks' place. That way, if they worried about him, they'd check the answering machine before heading out into the foul weather in search of him. Staying overnight at the Yoders' place would almost seem like a mini vacation. And he could dream of the future when he—*Gott* willing—owned the place. He smiled at the thought. *Jah*, that was what he'd do.

He stopped at the phone shanty at the end of the lane when he'd driven in, and left a message. Hopefully, *Mamm* wouldn't worry about him. Ten minutes later, he pulled into the drive. He led Strider to an empty stall in the barn, then filled a bucket with water and offered the horse some grain he kept stored in the corner.

He stood looking toward the house, waiting for a break in the rain. After a few minutes, he realized he might not get one. As a matter of fact, it was coming down even harder than when he'd pulled in. He was just glad he'd been able to arrive before the lightning struck. Now that Strider was securely in the barn, he'd settle in for the night. He'd have to wait until the rain died down a little bit to check the gutters.

He wished he'd thought to bring an umbrella. It certainly would have made his escape to the house a bit more pleasant. And dry.

Silas pushed the door open and immediately removed his boots. He paused for a moment, midstride as he walked through the living room. Had he heard something or was it just his imagination? It was difficult to determine above the rain pounding on the metal roof. He'd always loved the sound. How many nights had he fallen asleep to it?

He reached for the lantern on the table. Except it wasn't there. He could have sworn that he'd left it in the same place he always did—not that he'd ever really swear. As he allowed his eyes to adjust to the dim interior, he noticed something peculiar. Faint light seeped from the bedroom door, which seemed to be cracked open. The hairs on his arms raised. Was someone inside the house?

His heart began pounding. Who could be here? Dan Yoder hadn't said he was returning, so it must be an intruder. He quietly tiptoed toward the bedroom door, then put his ear to the crack. Sure enough, someone or something was in that bedroom.

All at once, he forced the door open and burst into the room. "What are you doing here?"

"Ah!" A young woman, who stood in only her undergarments, quickly pulled the bed quilt around herself.

*Jah*, that had been a mistake. Too bad he'd realized it too late. His face burned. "I...I'm sorry...you just...uh, *jah*...I'll...I'll just go...out." He turned around as quickly as he'd entered. *Oh, man. What have I done?*

Silas paced the living room, trying to determine his next course of action. Had he *really* just burst in on a woman while she was changing? *Ach! Dummkopp.*

A few moments later, the woman—fully dressed now—walked into the room. "I'm sorry that you..." She shook her head. "This is a little awkward."

He nodded. *Jah*, it certainly was. He had no words.

"My daughter and I were out driving in the storm. She needed to use the facilities, so we stopped in here, thinking someone would be home. We'd only planned to use your restroom and then be on our way to search for a hotel, but they'd sent out flash flood warnings and my GPS lost its signal. And frankly, I don't even know where we are." She glanced toward one of the bedrooms. "My daughter is sleeping already. But we can leave if you'd like us to...uh, Mr. Yoder."

"Oh, I'm not Dan Yoder. My name is Silas Miller. I live down the road a spell. I'm tending Yoder's farm while he's gone."

"Oh, okay. When will he be back? Do you think he'd mind if we stayed the night? I didn't want to assume, but we really have no place to go."

"Not sure if he's coming back." He lifted his hat and plowed his fingers through his hair. What should he do? He didn't want to kick this woman and her daughter out in the storm. But if they stayed here, where would *he* spend the night? He didn't relish the thought of sleeping in the barn with the mice.

"Do you want us to go?"

*In a word, yes.* But he wouldn't say that out loud. How could he kick them out when they didn't have any place to go? And in this storm. "The nearest hotel is about fifteen miles south of here." He shifted from one foot to the other. "But I reckon it would be all right if you stayed here."

She sighed, and he could almost feel her relief. "You don't know how glad I am to hear you say that. I'm not that confident driving in this kind of weather. I'm dreading going back out into that storm."

*Jah*, so was he. But he'd have to do it anyway. Because there was no way he was staying in this house with a woman present.

You can continue reading *The Trespasser* here: https://books2read.com/u/bpwAkE in ebook, or you can order the **paperback** from your favorite retailer or order direct by requesting a mail order form at:

jebspredemann@gmail.com

or

Jennifer Spredemann
PO BOX 70
CROSS PLAINS IN 47017

It's not too late to subscribe to my newsletter! Get a FREE Amish story as my thank you gift when you sign up for my newsletter here: www.jenniferspredemann.com

Dear Reader,

Thank you for reading *The Newcomer*!

I hope you've enjoyed the story so far. If you haven't read the remainder of the books in this series, I urge you to continue reading to find out what the future holds for Silas, Kayla, Bailey, and other characters you're sure to fall in love with.

The next book in the series begins with Kayla driving cross-country to see if she can locate her daughter's father, Josiah Beachy. She is still unaware of the events that took place in Ocean City after her family's departure. From there, well, I'll just let you read for yourself what happens!

I loved writing this series and getting to know each of the characters, and I'm certain you will too. As my editor (who is not typically an Amish fiction reader) said, I think I want to go back and read through the series again.

I know I'm going to miss these characters, but the *wunderbaar* thing about books is that you can go back and visit your favorite characters and places again and again. If you have completed the series, I sincerely hope it has been a blessing!

To GOD be the glory!

Blessings in Christ,
Jennifer Spredemann
*Heart-Touching Amish Fiction*

P.S. Word of mouth is one of the best forms of advertisement and a HUGE blessing to the author. If you enjoyed this book and/or series, **please** consider leaving a review, sharing on social media, and telling your reading friends.

# A SPECIAL THANK YOU

I would like to express a *special* **thank you** to all my readers, who helped with the names in this book. To readers, **Julie Dahl** and **Dianna Nance**, thank you for suggesting the names "Ezra" and "Dorcas" for the Miller parents.

I'd like to take this time to thank everyone that had any involvement in this book and its production, including my Mom and Dad, who have always been supportive of my writing, my longsuffering Family—especially my handsome, encouraging Hubby, my Amish and former-Amish friends who have helped immensely in my understanding of the Amish ways, my supportive Pastor and Church family, my Proofreaders, my Editor, my Author friends, my wonderful Readers who buy, read, offer great input, and leave encouraging reviews and emails, my awesome Launch Team who, I'm confident, will 'Sprede the Word' about *The Newcomer*! And last, but certainly not least, I'd like to thank my *Precious LORD and SAVIOUR JESUS CHRIST*, for without Him, none of this would have been possible!

If you haven't joined my Facebook reader group,
you may do so here:
https://www.facebook.com/groups/379193966104149/

Made in United States
Troutdale, OR
09/28/2024

23190391R00130